US and
Uncle Fraud

OTHER YEARLING BOOKS YOU WILL ENJOY:

US and Uncle Fraud

Uncle Fraud

Lois Lowry

A Yearling Book

Published by
Dell Publishing Co., Inc.
1 Dag Hammarskjold Plaza
New York, New York 10017

Yearling® TM 913705, Dell Publishing Co., Inc.

ISBN: 0-440-49185-1

Reprinted by arrangement with Houghton Mifflin Company

Printed in the United States of America

First Yearling printing—October 1985

CW

This one is for my blue-eyed grandson,
James Michael.

US and
Uncle Fraud

1

laude's coming," my mother said in some surprise, looking up from the letter in her hands. "For Easter."

Father lowered the newspaper and looked up. He scowled. Then he picked the paper up again and turned a page quickly so that it made a whipping sound. But we were used to that. Father was the paper's editor, and each night he whipped through the pages, scowling, finding mistakes here and there. "Misplaced modifier," he would say, groaning, or "Inappropriate apostrophe." Sometimes he put his head into his hands in despair. He was always very fast, finding errors. But tonight he turned the flimsy pages more swiftly than usual while Mother watched. Finally he looked up again.

"Wasn't he just here? Wasn't he here last month?"

"Oh, Matt," Mother said, laughing. "It's been three years. He's never even seen Stephie."

She put the letter on the table beside her chair and leaned over to pick up my sister who was playing on the floor near her feet. Stephie was ready for bed, already in her pink flannel pajamas; she put her thumb into her mouth and curled into Mother's lap, twisting a strand of her own dark hair around the fingers of her other hand.

"You're going to meet your Uncle Claude," crooned Mother to Stephie, who sucked rhythmically on her thumb, her eyes half-closed. "Uncle Claude, Uncle Claude, Uncle Claude," Mother murmured, making a lullaby of it. Stephie's eyes closed and her thumb, glistening, dropped to her side. In her sleep her mouth moved, looking for the thumb, then relaxed.

Mother patted my sister's back. "I'll take her up to bed," she said softly. Then she turned to us. "Do you remember Claude?" she asked.

I tried. Three years ago I had been eight. Adults had come and gone in my life, but the men all seemed the same. I remembered women by what they wore, how they smelled and sounded, and what their secrets were. Mother's friend, Mrs. Mallory, wore black, and smelled of cologne; her husband had died of something mysterious called FUO, Fever of Unidentified Origin, my mother had explained to me mournfully. My aunts, Father's sisters, Florence and Jeanette, always dressed in billowing pastels — dresses that seemed incongruously like those worn by Stephie's dolls — but they walked heavily, with stomping noises, through our house, and their voices, too, were heavy and loud. Neither had ever married, and Mother had whispered to me that they disliked men, although in their odd, explosive way, they were fond of Father.

But I had no memories of sounds or secrets connected with Claude. I shook my head. "Is he good-looking?" I asked. Now that I was eleven and went to the movies almost every Saturday afternoon, I was interested in the *looks* of men. The dashing, sinister appearance of film villains appealed to me.

Mother chuckled. "Not handsome," she said, tilting her head as if to remember. "I'd call him *sweet*-looking, I guess."

I shrugged and looked back at the game of checkers that I was losing to my brother on the living room rug. "Sweet-looking" didn't sound very interesting.

Marcus jumped two of my men, removed them from the board, and kinged himself. He smirked at me and I glowered. Marcus was only ten, but he always won. I thought he cheated, but I could never catch him at it.

My older brother, Tom, stirred in his chair and rustled his section of the paper, the sports page. Tom was fourteen, and he seemed to be turning into Father. His voice was deepening; he had gotten glasses this year; he walked like Father, talked like Father, and shared Father's opinions about politics; and he had lately, to my chagrin, taken to calling me "Lulu" the way Father did, but with a patronizing kind of affection. My name, I reminded him often and haughtily, was Louise. When I said my own name aloud, I bounced it into three syllables, hoping that others would take up the affectation and that I could become "Louisa" in a gradual and surreptitious way.

Tom said, "I remember him. Good old Claude the Fraud." He said "fraud" in an exaggerated fashion, catching his lower lip with his top teeth to make the *f* and then filling his cheeks with air, blowing it out into the word so that the name seemed laughable and foolish. He and Father grinned at each other.

Mother shook her head, chuckling, and rose with Stephie in her arms. "He's arriving Friday," she said, "by train."

Father called after her as she carried Stephie up the stairs. "We don't have room, Hallie," he pointed out half-heartedly.

"He can have my room," I said, "and I'll sleep in Marcus's room." Then I added, "The way I do when Aunt Florence and Aunt Jeanette come to visit."

"At least there's only one of Claude," Father said, and lifted the newspaper again. "*My* relatives come in whole herds."

Marcus and I laughed. Florence and Jeanette were a pair, not a whole herd, but it did seem, when they came to visit, as if a disorganized army had arrived. Behind their broad pastel backs, Father called them Flotsam and Jetsam, even though Mother, giggling, told him again and again to shush.

There was only a half-day of school on Friday. Some of the kids groaned that they would have to spend the entire afternoon in church, mourning the death of Jesus. I mourned the death of Jesus in my own way, feeling uncomfortable and sad about the nails in his hands and feet. Once I had held my left hand flat against the workbench in the basement, and poked at it with a nail, just to see how it might feel. But it hurt too much, even just the nervous poking; I didn't have the courage to pierce my own skin. So I felt sorry for Jesus, but pleasantly smug that my family never attended church and that I wouldn't have to waste an entire school-free afternoon.

"I can do the sheets," I suggested to Mother, who was busily tidying the house with Stephie underfoot. "I can put clean sheets on my bed for Uncle Claude."

She hesitated. "Well," she said, "are you sure you can do a good job? Claude likes very tight corners."

"Of *course* I can."

"All right, then. I'll check it when you're done." She sighed, looking around at all that was left to do. Our house was always a mess. Mother's projects — sewing, knitting, embroidery, even a half-done watercolor at least a year old — were everywhere. Stephie's toys were scattered on the living room floor; Mother gathered them all into the laundry basket and set it on the stairs. Father's newspapers were in a tall stack beside his leather chair; she looked at it, shook her head, and left it there. Once she had put them all out with the trash and he had bellowed for days.

Marcus's ice skates still dangled by their laces from the coatrack in the hall, although the ice had been too thin for skating for nearly a month. Mother looked at them, frowning, then lifted them down by their laces and handed them to me.

"Put these in Marcus's room when you go up," she said. "And use the blue sheets. They're on the bottom shelf of the linen closet. Use pillowcases to match. And tight corners. Remember? Like in a hospital."

It was one of Mother's seeming non sequiturs. My tonsils had been removed in the hospital when I was five, but surely Mother knew I hadn't noticed how the bed was made. I went upstairs, deposited Marcus's skates on his bed, and found the blue company sheets. Carefully I remade my own bed for Uncle Claude, pulling the corners tight by crumpling all the excess fabric and stuffing it under the mattress. I smoothed the blanket the way Mother did; as an afterthought, I left a green Life Saver on the pillow, as a welcoming gift, and dusted the tops of the furniture with the used pillowcase before I tossed it into the laundry hamper.

Later in the afternoon, Stephie napped, waking at twilight with her face creased and her curls moist, just as my brothers came in, muddy and arguing noisily, from a ball game in the vacant lot.

"Is he here yet?" asked Marcus.

"Claude the Fraud?" Tom added. "Is Claude the Fraud here yet?"

"No," said Mother sharply. "And stop that. Don't you dare do that when he's here. You boys go upstairs now and wash. Change into clean clothes. Louise, get Stephie changed, would you? I'm going to start dinner. His train arrives at six."

"Is Father going to the train station for him?" Tom asked.

"No. Claude will walk from the station. He always does. It's only three blocks and he doesn't like to inconvenience anyone. Claude is a very considerate boy."

"Boy?" I asked in amazement. "Is Claude a *boy*?"

Mother turned on her way to the kitchen. She looked startled. "No," she said. "I guess not. Claude must be—well, let me think. He's a year younger than I am. That makes him thirty-five. Isn't that odd, that I always think of Claude as a boy?" She stood there a moment, as if she were surprised at her own mistake. Then she chuckled. "He's a *man*. I wonder why I forget that?"

The house was polished now, and gleaming; the toys were put away, and even Father's newspapers were patted into an evenly aligned stack. It seemed quiet, although I could hear Marcus and Tom still arguing, upstairs, about a controversial play in the infield. I took my sister up to her room and dressed her in pale blue overalls and a yellow sweater. She sat on my lap as I tied her high-topped shoes, and we looked out the window together, down the quiet street where the lights were beginning to appear in the windows of our neighbors' houses.

"Claude," I told Stephie. "Can you say 'Claude'?"

"Claude," Stephie repeated precisely and dutifully.

"Can you say 'Uncle Claude'?"

She shook her head and put her thumb into her mouth. I could see her grinning around the thumb. She could say it if she wanted to.

"Uncle Claude is Mommy's brother," I explained. "But he's a grown-up man. Do you know who Stephie's brothers are?"

She shook her head again, still grinning.

"Marcus and Tom, dummy," I told her. "You know that." She nodded, giggling, climbed from my lap, and scampered away. I sat alone in her room and watched from the window until my uncle arrived.

Uncle Claude was a disappointment at first. He wasn't at all handsome; he wasn't even, as Mother had suggested, sweet-looking, whatever that meant. He was — well, he was *nothing*. His face was like a face in my "learn-to-draw-people" book; it had all the correct features of a face, and in the right places, but it had nothing to distinguish it. Father's face had creases across the forehead and two pinch marks at the sides of his nose when he took his glasses off. Father had a line separating his chin into two parts, like a boulder that had been partially split during some prehistoric age; Mother called it a "cleft" and said it made Father unusually handsome.

Even Tom had a face that one could remember. When you saw Tom's face, much like Father's, even to the cleft chin, but without the creased forehead, you knew it was Thomas F. — for Frederick — Cunningham that you were looking at.

And Marcus, too. Marcus had freckles everywhere and a chicken pox scar by his right eyebrow; one of his front teeth was chipped, and he had a habit of poking the jagged place with his tongue when he was thinking.

But Claude's face was bland, like pudding with no nuts or raisins sprinkled in. It was smooth, with no lines or scars or freckles; and his hair was straight and dull, not streaked with gray like Father's or carefully combed and parted like Tom's. Certainly he had none of Marcus's wild curls.

He looked, I thought, like the turtle I had had once, with the same lipless, pleasant expression.

As the turtle had been, Uncle Claude would be boring, I decided. I shook his hand politely; at least he did not say, as my aunts always did, how tall I had grown.

Instead, he bowed slightly, and held my hand for a moment before letting it go. "There once was a girl named Louisa," he said in a solemn voice, "Who liked all the young men to tease her —"

I looked up at him, startled.

"I can't tell you the rest right now," he said. "It's rather risqué."

He let my hand go and winked at me.

"And you remember Marcus," Mother said, pushing my brother a little so that he, too, would shake hands. Grudgingly Marcus held out his hand.

Instead of shaking it, Uncle Claude leaned down and inspected Marcus's hand carefully. "Good," he said, after a moment. "No weapons. Sometimes a tiny one can be concealed very cleverly."

"What?" Marcus looked at his own hand, puzzled.

"That's the original purpose of handshaking," Uncle Claude explained. "So that strangers could indicate that they had no deadly weapons. Of course, with today's technology, a tiny poison dart could be concealed even in an open palm. I felt that I had to examine yours very carefully because, to be honest, you looked a little hostile. But your hand looks clean. I feel safe."

"It *should* look clean," Marcus said. "I just washed it." Then he held it out a second time and shook Uncle Claude's hand quite firmly. He grinned. Marcus liked to be thought dangerous.

"Me," said Stephie loudly. "My turn."

"This is Stephanie," Mother explained. "She's two-and-a-half."

Claude picked her up. "Two-and-a-half pounds?" he asked. "Or quarts? Quarts of pickles?"

"Pickles," giggled Stephie.

"Rhymes with tickles," announced Uncle Claude and wiggled his fingers under her arms until she shrieked with delight. Then he gave her a kiss on the cheek and put her down.

Tom and Father had settled down in the living room with the evening paper. If the President of the United States had come for a visit, Tom and Father would have settled down in the living room with the evening paper.

"Louise," Mother said, "and Marcus. Take Uncle Claude's things up to his room. Claude, I've put you in Louise's room — she'll sleep in with her brother."

"I don't mind," I told him quickly.

Claude indicated a shabby suitcase on the hall floor. "You'd better take that one, Marcus, because it's extremely heavy and I can see that you have exceptional muscles. This other one, Louise —" he indicated a small box beside it, encircled with a leather strap — "is not heavy, but the contents are priceless and fragile, so I hope you'll take excruciating care with it when you transport it to my room."

I picked it up very carefully. It was so light it felt empty.

Marcus tugged at the suitcase, but looked at the box I was holding. "What's in it?" he asked.

Uncle Claude had turned to go into the living room. "I admire that kind of direct questioning," he said to Marcus. "But you'll understand, I'm sure, that some direct questions just can't be given direct answers. The box contains secrets."

Marcus nodded importantly. "Oh," he said.

"And surprises," Claude continued, looking at me. I was still holding the box gingerly. "For certain children."

"Priceless and fragile?" I repeated, weighing the seemingly weightless box in my hands. "For *us*?"

"For certain children," Uncle Claude said again, very meaningfully. "More I cannot say."

From the living room, I could hear Father give a cynical snort as he turned a page of the paper. Marcus and I scurried up the stairs with Claude's things and laid them carefully on my bed. I went to my Life Saver hoard a second time and chose a red one — reds were my favorites. I placed it beside the green one on the pillow. My Life Savers were neither priceless nor particularly fragile; but if Uncle Claude had brought me a gift — and I was sure he had, there in the mysterious box — I wanted to offer something in return. Suddenly he seemed like an extraordinary uncle.

2

M y feet are cold," I whispered to Marcus, after we had curled up in the twin beds and turned out the light. "I wonder why only babies like Stephie get to have pajamas with feet in them. I could sure use some."

"What do you think's in that box?" Marcus asked, ignoring my feet.

I had been wondering the same thing, of course. "It doesn't weigh anything. Maybe money? Money's light, if it's dollar bills."

Marcus yawned. "Claude doesn't have any money. Father said he was down-and-out, as usual."

"He didn't say that to Claude, did he?" Father's hearty rudeness was notorious, and usually I was delighted by it. But I liked Uncle Claude; I didn't want him to be shamed by Father.

"No," Marcus said sleepily. "He said it to Mother. He asked Mother what Claude was doing here, and Mother said that he's just passing through, and Father said" — here Marcus assumed Father's gruff, deep voice — " 'Just passing through looking for a handout again. He's down-and-out, as usual.' "

I snuggled deep into the bed with my arms around the pillow. "Well, so what?" I said. "He still has secret stuff in the box, and he said it's priceless and fragile. Probably he's been carrying it around for a long time, waiting to bring it to us, and even if he's down-and-out, he wouldn't sell it because it was for us."

Marcus didn't answer.

"Right?" I asked, after a moment's silence.

But he still didn't answer.

"Marcus?" I whispered. I lifted my head to peer through the darkness at him. He was asleep, his mouth open, his breathing soft and deep.

I heard footsteps on the stairs. Mother and Father were coming up to bed; I could hear them talking quietly to each other. The door to Marcus's room opened and a stream of light from the hall cut a strip across the rug. I closed my eyes and forced my breathing into a regular, slow rhythm.

Mother pulled the blankets up around our shoulders and tucked them in. I heard her move away and check the window — open a bit to the cool early April air — and then the door closed quietly again.

I heard her go to Stephie's room, and I could imagine the same ritual, the rearranging of the blanket over my sister in her crib, the adjustment of the window, the tiptoeing away.

She didn't check on Tom. After a certain age, Mother said, people didn't like to be looked at while they slept. I still did. It was reassuring, pretending to be asleep and hearing her slippered feet pad through the room for a final check on my comfort.

I heard Mother and Father's door close, and after a few minutes, I heard the snap of their light switch and knew that now, too, their room was dark.

I listened. I wanted to hear Uncle Claude come upstairs. My room shared a wall with Marcus's, and I knew that through the wall I would hear him find the Life Savers on his pillow. Maybe I would hear him unfasten the strap on the small box and check its priceless, fragile contents.

But he didn't come. I could hear footsteps downstairs; I heard the refrigerator door open; I heard ice cubes being shaken from their tray and emptied into a glass. A faucet ran briefly. The footsteps came from the kitchen and went back into the living room. I heard the creak as Uncle Claude settled into Father's leather chair.

Marcus turned and sighed in his sleep. I stared at the ceiling, not at all tired, and wondered what Claude was doing downstairs.

Finally I turned the covers back and climbed out of bed. Marcus didn't stir. Barefoot, I crossed the room and went out into the dark hall. In the bathroom, a small nightlight glowed. I shivered in my flannel nightgown, blinked in the dim light, and tiptoed down the stairs.

At the foot of the stairs, I made my footsteps

heavier on purpose, so that I wouldn't startle Uncle Claude. I didn't want him to think that I was a sneak.

But he wasn't startled at all. He glanced over, lifting his eyes from a magazine in his lap, and smiled.

"Louise Amanda," he said. "You're a night owl, just like me. I could tell that the minute I met you."

"How?"

"Large pupils in your eyes," he explained gravely. "And those are a sign that you can travel in dim light. I have the same characteristic."

I peered into his eyes, and he was right. His eyes were brown, like mine, with large black pupils.

"Nocturnal beasts we are," he said.

"How did you know my middle name?" I asked him. "I never tell it to anybody."

"Louise Amanda," he repeated. "It could almost be one word: Louisamanda. The Louisamanda Purchase, 1803, a date from history. Or it could be the name of a museum. Do you know that outside of Copenhagen there is a museum called the Louisiana? The man who built it named it for his wives. He married only people named Louise. He married one Louise after another.

"It's at the edge of the Baltic Sea," he went on, and picked up his glass and sipped. A bottle of Father's whiskey was on the table beside him.

"Have you been there? At the edge of the Baltic Sea?" I asked him.

He nodded. He refilled his glass from Father's

whiskey. "Yes," he said, "I've been there. Once I told him that he should name his museum Louis-amanda. But he became belligerent, and said I should build my own museum. He was right, of course. You can't put names to other people's things. I apologized to him for my suggestion and slunk away, duly chastened." He sipped again.

I sat down on the couch, opposite Father's chair. "How did you know my middle name?" I asked again.

"Thomas Frederick Cunningham," Claude said, "your ubiquitous older brother, was named for his great-grandfather, Thomas Frederick Newbold, who served without distinction in the army during World War I.

"That was my grandfather," Claude explained, taking another drink, "and therefore your brother's — and your — great-grandfather."

He refilled the glass again.

"Louise Amanda. Your great-grandmother. She was born Louise Amanda Taggart; she married Thomas Frederick Newbold, who served without distinction in the army; and she died at the age of forty-two, having given birth to six children, four of whom survived, one of whom was Marcus New-bold, who was your mother's father, and therefore mine. And so your very brash and freckled brother is named —"

He looked at me and waited for the answer.

"Marcus Newbold Cunningham," I said, and he nodded and sipped.

"But then there's Stephie," I pointed out. "Who had Stephie's name?"

"Stephanie Ann Cunningham," Claude sighed. "Who knows? Your parents had lost their sense of heritage by then. Your sister received a name with no history. She will survive it, I expect. I have."

"Doesn't your name have a history?"

"I am attempting to create one for it," Claude said gloomily. "What time is it, Louisamanda?" He looked at his wrist and squinted, but couldn't seem to focus on his watch.

I could see the hall clock from where I sat. "Almost eleven," I told him.

"The night is young," Claude muttered. "If you were twenty-eight years old, I would invite you to join me at the opera."

I laughed aloud. "There's no opera in this town," I pointed out.

"We would go to London," he said, and picked up the whiskey bottle. He held it against the light and shook it from side to side. It was empty. "If only you were twenty-eight years old, I would take you to London in the morning."

Suddenly I was sleepy. I yawned.

"Uncle Claude," I asked shyly, "what's in the box?"

He stared blankly at me.

"The priceless, fragile secret in the box I took upstairs," I reminded him.

"Go to bed, Louisamanda," Uncle Claude said. "I thought you were a creature of the dark, but suddenly your pupils have diminished in size. They've turned to sinister slits."

I rose immediately, embarrassed, and headed for the stairs. "I'm sorry," I said. "I shouldn't have asked."

He squinted at me. "Are you duly chastened?"

I wasn't certain what he meant, but I nodded. "Yes," I said.

"Good. I'll tell you in the morning what's in the box. I'll tell you and your freckled brother — Marcus Newbold Cunningham — but no one else. Now then: Do you know how to say good night in three different languages?"

"No."

"One. *Bonne nuit.* That's French. Say it."

"Bonne nuit," I said.

"God natt. Swedish."

"God natt," I repeated.

"Gute Nacht. German." He leaned back in his chair and closed his eyes.

"Gute Nacht," I said, but he didn't hear me. *"Bonne nuit. God natt. Gute Nacht,"* I murmured, memorizing as I went up the stairs and back to Marcus's room.

"I want you and Marcus to show me your town, Louise," Uncle Claude said at breakfast. "If you don't mind, of course."

Tom glanced at him suspiciously through his metal-rimmed glasses. Usually Tom was the one selected for such tasks. Tom could recite the history of our little town, pointing out landmarks: the grave of the World War I flying ace, the place where the river had crested during the flood of 1913, the site recently selected for the new library to be built next year.

But Claude smiled pleasantly back at my older brother. "I remember when I was passing through three years ago, Thomas, and you showed me around. Did a remarkable job of it, too, for a boy who was then no more than — what? Thirteen?"

"Eleven," Tom said, going back to his scrambled eggs. "Three years ago I was only eleven. Same as Louise is now."

"Is that a fact? I'm amazed. I could have sworn you were at least thirteen, giving an authoritative tour the way you did."

Marcus and I grinned at each other. Tom was known for his air of authority — he always had been — and we were sure that Uncle Claude was needling him. But Tom nodded, taking Claude's comment as a compliment. "Not much has changed," he said, "but the kids can show you around this time. If you have questions you can ask me when you get back."

"Would you mind taking the baby along?" Mother asked. "She could use the fresh air."

Marcus and I groaned in unison. Stephie was such a pest; she dawdled and whined. But Claude reached across the table to tickle her under her chin. "Want to go for a walk, Picklepuss?" he asked. "Are your legs up to a sturdy hike?"

Stephie dimpled and nodded, orange juice on her upper lip.

Upstairs, pulling sweaters over our heads in his room, I said to Marcus, "He said he'd tell us what's in the box. He said he'd tell us this morning. Only you and me."

Marcus took his baseball cap from the top of a lamp and pulled it down over his mountain of curls. "When?" he asked. "When did he say that?"

"Last night. I couldn't sleep last night, and real late, I went downstairs and talked to him."

"Liar. You went to sleep before I did."

"I am not a liar. Ask him. We sat downstairs and drank whiskey, and he told me he'd been at the edge of the Baltic Sea."

"*You* drank whiskey? I'm going to tell Father. It'll stunt your growth. You'll end up a midget if you drink whiskey before you're grown-up. What did it taste like?"

"I didn't drink it, stupid; Claude drank it. Father's whole bottle of whiskey was gone when I went up to bed."

"That's why Father was so mad this morning," Marcus said knowingly. "I heard him tell Mother that her brother is a lush."

"Well," I said slowly, "at least he's been at the edge of the Baltic Sea. I don't know anyone else in the whole world who's been there."

"And he's got that box full of stuff for us, and this morning he's going to tell us what it is, right?"

"Right."

"Louise! Marcus! Are you ready?" Mother was calling from the foot of the stairs. We ran down.

"Here," she said and handed me a dollar. "Stop at the grocery store on your way home and buy a dozen eggs. Make sure they're white ones, for dyeing. A dozen's enough, don't you think?"

Marcus calculated. "That's four each for me and Louise and Stephie. Tom says he's too grown-up now for Easter eggs, the jerk."

Mother sighed. "Twelve's enough, then. Be sure to hold Stephie's hand. And show Uncle Claude where they've pointed the brick on the bank, and, let's see, maybe he'd be interested in the window display at Baumen's Department Store —"

Claude appeared, with his shabby jacket on, and interrupted her. "Right," he said, "we mustn't miss that. And we'll check out all the churches to see how they've decorated for Easter." He was grinning.

"Claude," Mother said, in the same chiding voice she used with Father, "stop that. Don't be disrespectful." But she was grinning back at him.

Holding Stephie by her hands, we swung her down over the porch steps and started off.

3

Our town was not a town of distinction. It was like a hundred — maybe a thousand, maybe a million — other small towns, built a century ago along the eastern bank of a sluggish, tan river with an Indian name.

Like all those other towns, it had a main street lined with stores and banks, a movie theater, a newspaper, a couple of gas stations, and a post office. There was a library, small and turreted, on a side street; next year they would build a new, expanded one, and the little Gothic library in which I had grown into a literate eleven-year-old would be torn down to make way for a parking lot.

There was the Town Hall, which contained the police station and small jail, and the hospital in which we (all but Stephanie) had had our tonsils removed. The elementary school that Marcus and I attended was a squat brick building near the center of town, an easy walk from our house. Tom attended the junior high; it, and the senior high beside it, were "regional schools" five miles from town. Yellow buses collected Tom and the others from the corners of neighborhood streets, and the same buses navigated the flat, patchwork countryside to pick up the "farm kids" — the kids with German, Slavic, and Scandinavian names — waiting at the mailboxes that dotted the winding country roads.

On the other side of the river, reached by an impressive bridge, the teacher's college sprawled over a brown, almost treeless hill. On Saturday afternoons in the fall, if the wind came from the west, as it usually did, we could hear the exuberant cheers or distressed groans of the crowd as the college team fought its way toward a Class C football championship. Father's paper paid little attention to the sports events at the college; the headlines came from the better teams of the universities that lay many miles away.

Our town was divided into neighborhoods by economic class: the poor neighborhood, the middle, and the rich; we were in the middle, always had been, always would be, and we neither looked down on the poor nor aspired to be part of the rich. No one did.

We walked past the imposing Presbyterian Church that stood at the end of our block.

"Yesterday," I said to Uncle Claude, who had lifted Stephie to his shoulders and was carrying her there, "all the church bells were ringing. It was before your train got in. Yesterday was Good Friday; did you know that?"

Claude, striding along the sidewalk with Stephie holding both ears like handles, glanced down at me. "Of course I knew that," he said. "In the middle of the afternoon, my train slowed down and gave seventeen long, penitential blasts of its whistle. We were passing a dairy farm at the time, and four hundred cows fell to their knees and bowed their heads."

"Moooo," crooned Stephie from her knobby-shouldered perch.

Marcus had lagged behind to squat and retie his shoe. I waited for him while Stephie and Uncle Claude sauntered on ahead, mooing together.

"Ask him, Louise," ordered Marcus. "Ask him about the box."

"I *can't*. He told me he'd only tell you and me. So I can't ask him when stupid Stephie's there."

Marcus frowned. "Great," he said sarcastically. "So we have to spend the whole morning showing him around this dumb town."

I shrugged. We plodded ahead to where Claude had turned and was waiting for us, Stephanie still attached to his shoulders like a giggling growth.

We were on the corner of our residential street, where it joined Main Street, and we had a choice of going north or south. "Which way would you like to go, Uncle Claude?" I asked politely. "If we turn left, you could see the school that Marcus and I go to. Or if we turn right, there's the Town Hall in about two blocks. If you stand behind the Town Hall, you can look across the river to the college."

"I'm sure you go to a fine school," Uncle Claude said, "since you've both turned out to be such fine, intellectual people. But frankly, I've seen enough schools to last me a lifetime. And as for town halls —" He made a face.

Marcus and I both grinned. We felt the same way about the Town Hall. But we couldn't think of much else to show him. It simply wasn't a very interesting town.

"That's it!" Claude said suddenly. "I couldn't hear you very well, because I have these human earmuffs on, but I could read your lips, and you're absolutely right."

Marcus and I looked at each other. Neither of us had said a word.

Claude pried Stephie's grip loose from his ears. "My dear," he said to her, "do you have large pockets in those overalls?"

"No," Stephie said. She clutched the collar of his jacket to steady herself on his shoulders.

"Well then," Claude told her, "it's a good thing I loosened your grip. In two more minutes, my ears would have fallen off, and without large pockets to carry them home in, we would have had to leave them right here on the sidewalk. Perhaps a large dog would have come along and had them for din-

26

ner, but then what would hold my hat on when winter comes?"

Marcus and I both looked automatically at the sidewalk, picturing detached ears lying there like dead oak leaves in October.

"Now," Claude went on, "I believe what I understood your moving lips to suggest was this: that you will show me the most interesting, exciting, dangerous, *secret* thing in your town. Something that very few people know about. Are you two in agreement about what that thing is to be? Consult with each other and decide before we set off."

My imagination soared. Every child knows of dangerous secret places, and each has a favorite. I knew that Marcus's was the ladder of the water tower on the south side of town; he had climbed it once almost to the top. He had walked the bridge across the river, too, with his friends: something we had been sternly forbidden to do. I was afraid of heights, so I had shared few of Marcus's secret places. But I had my own.

One of my friends from school was the daughter of a professor at the college. She had told me that in the Science Building, there on the hill across the river, if someone boosted you to a certain windowsill, you could peer into a lab and see dead babies floating in jars of fluid. Peering at the dead babies would have been my choice, but to get there we would have had to walk the bridge, something I was unwilling to do.

Marcus looked at me slyly. He had been pondering the choices too. "Leboffs'?" he suggested.

I nodded. It was the perfect choice, one of the secret places Marcus and I shared: a short walk, no perilous heights, a true secret, and a valid danger; but there was still an obvious problem.

"Stephie will tell on us," I pointed out.

"We'll just tell Stephie that we're showing Uncle Claude where the rich people live," Marcus whispered. "She can't even talk well enough yet to tell Mother anything more than that. Heck, *we* can tell Mother that — that we showed the Leboffs' house to Uncle Claude. She'll never know the rest."

I nodded in agreement. He was right. Together we turned back to Uncle Claude, like two conspirators.

"This way," I said. "We turn left for a block, and then we turn right, up that street over there."

Now he and Stephie followed us. "Horsie!" Stephie cried, and he trotted a bit, jouncing her up and down.

Although we had only three blocks to walk, we were moving from one world to another: from the world in which we lived, in our rambling shingled house, the world of houses like ours, with back yards and porches and hammocks and fences draped with honeysuckle in summer, to the more elegant, more austere world of the mansions built where the river bank was steep.

These were the homes of the people who had founded our town, families who had been there for a century. There were not many of them, and they were not among our friends; their children attended our schools only until they were twelve or so, and then they were sent east to boarding school. There had been an Evelyn Leboff in the grade above Tom, but she was gone now, to a school in Connecticut; and in Marcus's fifth-grade class there was a solemn, spectacled boy named Francis Hartmann, who lived here on what we called "The Riverbank." He was brought to school each day by his father's driver, and he never invited anyone home to play after school. That was simply the way it was.

All of the houses on The Riverbank — there were only seven — were grand estates by our standards, fortresses of massive stone set far back on sculptured lawns and in some cases surrounded by forbidding walls and gates. But the Leboffs' house was the grandest. When, in third grade, our class had turned a page in our geography books to reveal a photograph of something labeled "A Norman Castle," a murmur had passed through the room. "The Leboffs' house," we had all whispered. I had squinted at the page and pictured Evelyn Leboff, then a tall, bony girl with long braids, strolling beside the moat.

There was no moat at the Leboffs' house, and, in truth, it was not so much a Norman castle as it was a miniature version of one. It had the same stone turrets, the same massive door, but they were all condensed to a scale suitable for human life —

though certainly a different form of life from the one we knew.

Uncle Claude stood at the end of the long gravel driveway, with Stephie still on his shoulders, and whistled.

"Now that," he said, after his admiring whistle had expired, "is what I call a house. What do you call it, Miss Picklepuss?" He tilted his head and looked up at my little sister.

"House," she said solemnly. "*Big* house."

"Come on," Marcus said and started up the wide drive.

"Well now, Marcus the Newbold," Uncle Claude said, laughing, "I've clean forgot to bring my engraved calling cards. And I never go calling on royalty without my engraved calling cards."

"It's okay," I said. "Come on. They're not home."

Marcus was already partway up the drive. After a moment, Claude lifted Stephie from his shoulders and set her down on the driveway. She whimpered a little and held her arms up.

"I'll give you a ride back home," Claude said. "But for now I need a rest. My muscles are crying out. Listen: Can you hear them?" He knelt beside Stephie and put his shoulder to her ear. She listened, the way she always listened to Father's gold watch. Then she nodded.

"Quite a racket, isn't it?" Claude said and stood back up. "All those tiny muscle voices calling, 'We need a little rest, please!'"

Stephie nodded again, grinned, and took his hand. We started up the driveway.

"The Leboffs go to Europe every spring," I explained to Uncle Claude. "They leave the fifteenth of March, and they don't come back until June fifteenth."

"Louisamanda," he said, "I know you are a very precocious person, but you're overlooking something. A house like this has servants. Now I know that footmen and chambermaids died out with the Tyrannosaurus, but, even so, there's going to be a housekeeper in there, and I have a very strong suspicion that at this very moment she is looking through the windows at us, phoning the police station, and announcing: 'There is a band of Visigoths and Huns storming my driveway. Please come and pour boiling oil from the tower.'"

I laughed and shook my head. "The housekeeper is Mrs. Shaw, and every year from March fifteenth to June fifteenth she goes to Kansas City and visits her daughter, who has a fatherless child and a severe skin problem that causes her torments of itching." I was especially proud of that bit of gossip, which came from my mother, who had heard it from her friend Mrs. Mallory.

"Torments of itching?" Uncle Claude asked in amazement. *"Torments of itching?* How do we know it's not contagious? How do we know this entire driveway is not crawling with itching germs that have been brought here from Kansas City?"

He stamped his left foot hard on the gravel. "There. I think I got one," he said.

Stephie laughed and stamped her foot. "Me, too," she said. "I got one, too."

Marcus was waiting for us under the portico at the end of the driveway, where it curved around for cars. "Hurry up," he called.

"And there's no one else here, once Mrs. Shaw has gone to Kansas City to visit her itching daughter?" Uncle Claude asked. He was looking up at the massive house.

"No. And we can — well, wait. I'll let Marcus tell you."

When we reached the place where Marcus stood waiting, he beckoned for us to follow and turned to head for the back of the house. I had done this with Marcus before, so I knew where he was going. But Uncle Claude held back.

"Marcus," he said, "you are my good and trustworthy friend. But I am not going to go one step farther until you explain where you're taking me. I will plant my feet right here in this ostentatious driveway, and they will take root. I will become part of the shrubbery. They will have to prune me every fall and sprinkle bone-meal fertilizer over my shoes."

"Me, too," Stephie said, and she planted her feet.

Marcus sighed. "My friend from school," he explained in a loud whisper, "Kenny Stratton? His father is the Leboffs' driver. When they're here, I mean. He takes care of their cars, and he drives the

Leboffs everywhere. The cars are over there." Marcus pointed beyond the house to the side, where an extension of the driveway led to a large structure that had once been a carriage house and was now converted to a garage.

Uncle Claude looked and nodded. "Duly noted," he said.

"And when the Leboffs are away, like right now, Kenny Stratton's father takes care of the house. He checks it every night at six."

"Promptly at six? You're sure of that? He doesn't sometimes lose track of the time and come at—" Uncle Claude glanced at his watch—"eleven A.M.?"

"No," Marcus said impatiently. "He won't be back till this evening. So in the meantime we can look around, and no one will know."

"Well," Uncle Claude said, "I guess I could go along with that. I expect that from the back of the house you can look out over the river. We could pretend it's the Rhine. Do you feel like being a Rhine Maiden, Louisamanda?"

I didn't know what a Rhine Maiden was. But I nodded. I waited to see if Marcus would go on to reveal the rest.

Marcus moved ahead, through an opening in a hedge, and along a flagstone path that led into an area deeply shadowed by trees beside the towering gray walls of the house. We followed him, Stephie clinging tightly to Claude's hand and me bringing up the rear.

When the trees and shrubbery parted to open onto the vast lawn that ended at the steep riverbank, we stopped and looked with awe at the view. In April, with the runoff from melted snow, our slow, unimpressive river was turgid, deep brown in color, and punctuated with foamy whirlpools and woody debris. By midsummer it would be listless and lethargic again. But today it roared and churned.

Marcus didn't bother admiring the dangerous grandeur of the river. "Wait here for a minute," he commanded and disappeared.

"Where's that small Visigoth off to now?" Claude asked.

Well, it was Marcus's secret, but I decided that I would tell it anyway.

"He knows where Mr. Stratton keeps the key," I whispered. "We can go inside."

4

In a moment Marcus was back, a metal ring with a large key dangling from it in his hand. "It's always there," he announced, "on a little hook behind the third step to the back door."

But Uncle Claude was shaking his head in a decidedly negative way. "My good man," he said to Marcus, "you've shown enormous bravery and a definite devious cunning that is to be respected. But do you know what would happen if we used that key and entered this castle?"

"Nothing would happen," Marcus said with assurance. "I've done it before. So has Louise. And Kenny Stratton. He's the one who showed us where the key is kept, and —"

I interrupted him. "We don't touch anything," I explained. "We just *look*. There's all this fancy furniture, and paintings, and one of those giant pianos with the top that opens up, and — well, there's just all this stuff."

"A pool table," Marcus added. "We don't even touch that. We just walk around. Nothing happens."

"From that side," Uncle Claude said, pointing to the north, "the Militia would come. From over there —" now he pointed south — "the Gendarmes. In the meantime, large artillery would be lining up in front of the house, commanded by generals. We would be completely outnumbered, and we would be captured — though we would fight nobly, of course — and *then* —"

"Uncle Claude," I said, laughing, "nothing would happen. Honest."

But Stephie's eyes were wide. "What then?" she asked.

"Well," Claude said in a mournful voice, "do you see those four sycamore trees there, at the end of the lawn?"

We all looked and nodded.

"We would be tied there, one to each tree. I expect they would offer us blindfolds. Myself, I would refuse a blindfold. What about you, Marcus?"

Marcus nodded solemnly. "I'd refuse," he said.

"They would offer us each a last cigarette," Claude said, staring at the four sycamore trees. "Now I don't smoke. But I think I would probably accept that cigarette. Just as a gesture, you understand. What about you, Louisamanda?"

"Well, yes, okay, I'd accept a cigarette, I suppose."

"We'd stand there, tightly tied, bravely puffing on those final cigarettes, and then they would ask each of us if we had a last statement to make. Mine would be something slightly scornful, I think. Mine might be: '*Noblesse oblige*.' That's French. What about you, Marcus? What would you say?"

Marcus felt the edge of his chipped tooth nervously with his tongue. "Geronimo," he said. "Would that be okay, do you think?"

"Perfect," Claude said, nodding. "Louisamanda?"

I thought frantically. "'Onward, Christian Soldiers'? Is that all right?"

Claude beamed at me. "Incredible. It has just the right patronizing air of scornfulness. I wish I'd thought of it myself. Now: Stephie? What would you say?"

Stephie's chin was puckered. "I don't want a cigarette," she whimpered.

Uncle Claude picked her up. "Good for you," he said, patting her on the back. "You're a much better person than the rest of us. I think they'd probably untie you and let you run home. But Marcus. And Louise." He looked at us grimly. "You know what would come next, don't you?"

"Firing squad," Marcus muttered.

We all — except Stephie, who had her face buried in Claude's shoulder — looked once more at the row of death trees. None of us said anything for a moment.

Then Claude handed Stephie to me, and she wound her arms tightly around my neck. "Women and children stay here," Claude said. "Marcus and I will return the key to its place."

They were back in a minute, Claude's arm across Marcus's skinny shoulders. "Now," he announced, "we will beat a retreat."

"It's almost lunch time anyway," Marcus said.

"The eggs!" I remembered suddenly. "We have to stop at the store. I told Mother I'd buy eggs to dye for Easter."

We started down the driveway, and Claude lifted Stephie, who was cheerful again, to his shoulders once more. He was silent, and it looked as if he were thinking. Finally, when we were nearing Main Street, he said, "After lunch, Marcus and Louise, I will tell you what's in the box. We will have a *tête-à-tête*. That's French for secret meeting."

"Stephie," Mother said, untying my sister's bib, "after your nap we'll dye the eggs so that the Easter Bunny can hide them tonight."

Stephie nodded happily. At two-and-a-half she had no idea who the Easter Bunny was, or wasn't, but she was agreeable to anything that sounded like fun.

"I'll take her upstairs for her nap," Marcus volunteered. He had raced through lunch, slurping his vegetable soup and demolishing a tuna sandwich in four bites. "When's our secret meeting?" he asked, turning to Claude, who was still sipping coffee at the kitchen table.

"In a few minutes," Claude answered. "One o'clock sharp, in my bedroom. Excuse me," he added, looking at me apologetically, "I meant, of course, *Louise's* bedroom."

Marcus disappeared upstairs, holding Stephie by the hand. I took my own plate to the sink, rinsed it, and started off after them. But I stopped in the hall when I overheard Mother speak in a soft, firm voice to my uncle.

"Claude," she said, "don't you go filling their heads with nonsense."

I could hear his chuckle, and the sound of liquid as he poured more coffee from the pot into his cup. "They are *born* with their heads full of nonsense," he said. "Don't you know that that's what distinguishes mankind from the animal world?"

I could hear Mother sigh. "Claude," she said.

"Just think about it. A cat — now a cat will go off to a corner of the garage and have its kittens. A dog gives birth to puppies under the porch, or on the floor of a closet, surrounded by wet galoshes. Am I right or am I wrong?"

"You're right," Mother acknowledged.

"Now why do you think a human being like yourself — when you're expecting a baby — and only one usually, mind you, not a litter — dashes off to a hospital to be surrounded by doctors and nurses and anesthesia? You did that, didn't you, when your children were born?"

"Of course I did," Mother said. "It's safer. And easier."

"Exactly," Claude announced triumphantly. "It is more difficult to give birth to a human child because a human child has a *large head*. Are you following me?"

Mother started to laugh. "Yes," she said. "And the head is —"

"Right! Large because it is cram-chock-full of nothing but *nonsense*."

"I don't think my children are filled with nonsense," Mother said a little defensively.

"Look at your youngest," Claude said. "Look at Stephie."

"All right. What about her? Stephanie's a sweet little girl."

"Of course she is. But she's full of nonsense. The Easter Bunny. Her head is full of the Easter Bunny. She was born with the Easter Bunny in her head. Eventually you'll have to start replacing that. What are you going to replace it *with*?"

Mother didn't answer. I could hear the clink of coffee cups.

"Now," Claude said, as if he hadn't expected her to reply, "let's take a look at your oldest. Where *is* Tom, by the way?"

"Down at the office with his father. Matt always works on Saturday, and Tom spends all his time with him, at the paper, when he's not in school. Now that's not nonsense, Claude. Tom is a nice boy. He's a very responsible boy. He wants to be a newspaper-man like his father."

"My point exactly. There is not one iota of non-sense left in Tom's head. Somehow it was replaced with responsibility. Does Matt have any more bourbon hidden away, by any chance?"

"No," Mother said. "It's the middle of the day, Claude, for heaven's sake."

"No harm in asking. Now, where was I? Yes: Louise and Marcus."

I cringed, standing there silently in the hall. I wasn't at all sure I wanted to hear myself discussed. But I stayed and listened.

"What do you want for them?" Claude asked my mother.

"I'm not sure what you mean," she said slowly. "I want the best for them, of course."

"I know you do," Claude said. "And Hallie, don't you see what the best is? It's not newspapers. It's not this dull town by this tired river. Hallie, don't you remember when you and I were chil-dren?"

She laughed. "Yes. You were full of nonsense, Claude, and you still are."

"*Dreams*, Hallie. I was full of dreams."

She was silent. Finally she said, "What have they brought you? Nothing."

"Ah, Hallie, don't say that, not to me. I still pur-sue them. That's why I'm a traveling man — always will be. Nothing wrong with that."

"No," she sighed, "I guess not. But I don't want you filling my children's heads with craziness, Claude."

I could hear his chair scrape the floor as he pushed it back and stood up. "Dreams, Hallie. I'm simply putting dreams into their heads."

I scampered silently up the stairs, out of sight, when I heard Claude's footsteps in the hall.

5

Claude joined Marcus and me in my bedroom just as the clock in the hallway struck one. His suitcase was on the window seat, closed, and beside it was the small box, also closed and still sealed with its strap. My bed was neatly made. The green and red Life Savers were gone.

I wanted to get credit for the gift. "I see you ate the Life Savers I left for you," I said to Claude.

He looked puzzled for a moment, then glanced at the pillow where I had left them, and finally rolled his eyes in horror. "Life Savers?" he asked. "You mean they were candy?"

"Of course," I said. "You know what Life Savers are."

"My dear Louisamanda," he said, heaving a huge sigh, "my life is such that I cannot trust anything. Imagine entering an unfamiliar house, a house I have not visited for three years, so that I no longer knew if the inhabitants were friends or enemies.

Imagine finding —" he hesitated, and then spoke in a whisper, "— *edible objects* on my pillow."

I giggled. "I only meant them as a sort of present," I said.

"What a relief to hear that," he said, shaking his head. "I just couldn't be certain. The colors seemed meaningful — well, you can imagine."

"What color were they?" Marcus asked.

"You tell him, Louisamanda," Claude said. "I can hardly bring myself to speak of it. The shock of finding them there was so great."

"They were red and green," I told Marcus.

"You realize what that signifies," Claude said.

Marcus frowned. "*Stop* and *Go*?" he suggested. "Like on traffic lights?"

Claude reached over and shook Marcus's hand firmly. "Good man," he said. "You have the kind of quick perceptions that may bring you fame someday."

"It means cherry and lime," I scoffed. "It doesn't have any other meaning."

Uncle Claude put his arm around my shoulders. "I like that, Louise," he said. "You are not a suspicious person like Marcus and me. My life has been so fraught — absolutely *fraught* — with sinister occurrences that I confess that I misconstrued your gift. I felt that it was a message of some sort: a message that I should *Stop*, or perhaps *Go*, and — well, here they are. I saved them as evidence."

He reached over, pulled open the drawer of the

little table beside my bed, and revealed the two Life Savers. "I am humbled by your generosity," he said, "and shamed by my suspicions."

"Uncle Claude," I told him, "I wanted to give you a present because you said that you had a present — you know, in your little box."

"Ah," Claude said, "the little box." He picked it up and turned it over carefully in his hands. "Have you two ever been to Russia?"

"No," Marcus and I said together, watching his slender hands curved around the box.

"Russia today," Claude said in a soft, slow voice, "is a gray place. You probably go to the movies on Saturdays, don't you?"

We nodded.

"Well, many of the movies you see are Technicolor: everything bright and clear, with music and singing and dancing and romance. Am I right?"

We nodded.

"But some of them are black and white: grainy, drab —"

"The mysteries," I said, "and spy movies."

"Well," Claude went on, "Russia is grainy and drab these days. But there was a time when Russia was a Technicolor place, all sunlight and glistening golden onion-shaped domes. Czars and czarinas, and music and dancing. And in that time —" He paused. He was telling it like a story, the kind of story that made you want to say, "Yes? Go on!"

We waited.

"In that time, Easter mattered. The Russian Easter. Now of course I'm not talking about your Easter Bunny —"

We grinned. Marcus poked me.

Claude grinned, too. "The Russian Easter was the biggest celebration of the year. The brightest clothes, the best food, the happiest music, and the most decorated eggs."

"They had eggs, too? Like ours?"

"Aha," Claude said. "You've hit on the essential difference. No, their eggs were not at all like yours. Maybe the eggs of the *peasants* were. But we're talking now about the eggs of the czars. There was a jeweler — the jeweler to the royal family — the man who made the *crowns*, you understand. And he began to make the most fabulous Easter eggs in the world."

"We make pretty good ones," Marcus said. "If you dip just one half in the dye real carefully, and then let it dry, and put the other half in another color —"

Claude held his hand up. "Wait, my man," he said. "I have no doubt that you make fine Easter eggs in your kitchen. But you must envision that I am talking now about crystal eggs, silver eggs, golden eggs — eggs encrusted with jewels: pearls, rubies, emeralds —"

"Diamonds?" I asked.

"Of *course* diamonds," Claude said. "The entire egg a work of art, an oval veritably encrusted with priceless gems. And inside the egg —"

Marcus made a face. "Egg yolk."

"No, no. Inside the egg, a hollow: a whole tiny world; and you can look in through one end and see it there, shimmering. A whole miniature ballet, perhaps: dancers on their toes, dressed like swans, twirling around a glittering lake —"

"I hate ballet," Marcus groaned.

"Well then, picture this: in another, a battlefield! An entire miniature army, complete with cannons, horsemen, generals; even, sad to say, the wounded and dead lying on the snow-covered ground."

"How could you get all that into an *egg*?" Marcus asked skeptically.

Claude shrugged. "That was the secret of the man who made them. If it had been easy, everyone would have made them. But they couldn't. Only this one man — and his secret died with him. Very few of these Russian eggs still exist, and they are guarded by armed guards."

His voice became a whisper, and he stroked the box in his hands. "As far as I know, I am the only person who has ever been able to smuggle them across the border successfully. Others have tried, of course, and failed. Their fates were horrifying."

I realized that I was chewing on my thumbnail, an old habit that I had been trying to curb.

"What happened to them?" Marcus asked, his eyes wide. Marcus loved hearing about horrible fates.

Claude didn't answer. He simply shook his head.

"Show us," I begged. "Open the box, Uncle Claude."

Now he smiled. "We must abide by the royal tradition," he said. "They must be hidden, and you must search."

"Oh, *Claude*," I groaned.

"When?" Marcus asked. "When will you hide them?"

"While you sleep. Tonight."

Mother was calling from the kitchen. "Louise! Marcus! Come and help me set up the dyes, would you? Stephie will be up soon and we'll dye the eggs."

"Well," I sighed, glancing again at the box. "I still wish you'd give them to us right now." I tried to look mournful, winsome, and worthy.

But Claude shook his head. "It's the rules, Louis-amanda," he said. "The best gifts are the ones you must search for. I'm really quite amazed that your mother hasn't taught you that."

We rose reluctantly and headed for the door. "You won't forget, will you, Uncle Claude?" Marcus asked. "After we're asleep tonight, you won't forget to hide them?"

Claude popped the green Life Saver into his mouth and grinned. "Never fear," he replied. *"Pas de peur,"* he added. "That's French."

"I think maybe he *is* a fraud, like Tom and Father said," Marcus muttered as we got ready for bed that night. "Don't you?"

"No," I said decisively. "He's just a —" I hesitated, not at all sure how I wanted to describe our

uncle; the conversation I had overheard between
Claude and Mother had puzzled me without chang-
ing my feelings toward him. "He's a dream-chaser,"
I said, finally.

Marcus made a face. "Look," he said. "Father
said that Claude is down-and-out. He doesn't have
any money. So why would he be carrying around
a box full of jewels? Why didn't he sell them, if
they're worth all that money, like he says?"

"Because he meant them for *us*! He brought
them all the way out of Russia at the risk of his life,
for us. You don't trade something like that for gro-
ceries or to pay the rent." Suddenly I remembered
something. "Marcus! Remember when Mrs. Bostwick died?"

"Yeah." Marcus looked at me. "Yeah, I do. Is it
the same, do you think?"

Mrs. Bostwick had lived down the street, a few
houses away from us. She had been an ancient,
disagreeable woman who rapped on her window-
pane angrily if we chased a misthrown ball or a
runaway kitten into her messy yard. Her lawn was
a tangle of uncut weeds, and her house was ravaged,
an eyesore of peeling paint and loose, dangling
shutters.

Finally, one winter she had died. Her death was
discovered only when a town official went to the
house to discuss her unpaid taxes. Father had written the story for the paper himself, and it was reprinted in papers all across the country.

She had died of malnutrition and of cold. The

oil company had stopped delivering oil when her bills had gone unpaid for a year, and she was found in the coldest part of February, lying in a bed, covered with layers of blankets, and wearing three sweaters and a shabby coat. There was no food in the house, none at all.

Yet the house, Father's article had pointed out, was filled with Oriental rugs worth a fortune and with antiques that, had they been sold, could have fed and housed her for years. There was a diamond ring in a jewelry box and a string of real pearls.

A niece had come from Chicago, after Mrs. Bostwick's death, and Father had interviewed her for the newspaper article. "We didn't know," the niece had said in dismay. "We had no idea. I guess she couldn't bring herself to sell anything. They were family things. She was very proud of her family things, and she was determined they would stay in the family."

Now Marcus and I thought about Mrs. Bostwick. "Claude could be like that," I pointed out. "Those Russian eggs are family things to him. He meant them for us so of *course* he wouldn't sell them. Anyway, Claude's not starving. He's not cold."

"Yeah." Marcus nodded, agreeing. "But I think it's crazy. I'm going to sell mine."

"Your egg? With the jewels and the army and cannons and everything? You'd *sell* it?"

"Sure. Maybe not till I'm older. When I'm old enough to have a car, that's when I'll sell it. Who wants a dumb egg, when you can have a car?"

"Boy, I'm not. I wouldn't sell mine, even for a car. I'm going to keep mine on that shelf in my room, the one where my horse statues are. I'm going to keep it forever, and then when I die my kids will have it. And I'll never sell it, even if I'm starving. You're a jerk, Marcus, if you sell yours for a stupid car."

"Well, I haven't decided yet," Marcus admitted. "I have to see it, first. Maybe I'll change my mind. Maybe I won't sell it."

We got into bed and pulled the covers up around us.

"We'll be the richest kids in this town," I whispered. "We'll be richer than Francis Hartmann, even."

"Yeah. Richer than Francis Hartmann." Marcus's voice was sleepy and satisfied.

"I wonder if he's hiding them right now, right this minute." I listened for footsteps in the hall, but the house was silent. I hugged my pillow and wondered where Claude would hide the fabulous eggs. The ordinary Easter eggs were always hidden in obvious spots — under the couch cushions and on top of books in the bookcase.

But these weren't ordinary. These were our whole future — Marcus's and mine — and like all priceless and fragile futures, they would not, I knew, be easy to find.

6

~~~~~~

Stephie was up first in the morning, as she usually was, except for Tom, who had gone off at dawn to deliver the Sunday papers. She scampered around downstairs in her pajamas, carrying her bright-colored Easter basket filled with garish pink grass.

"Red!" Stephie crowed, taking an egg from its hiding place on the windowsill behind the curtains. "A red one!"

Marcus and I hung back and watched. Suddenly, to both of us, the game seemed a thing for babies. Yet last year we had joined in, dashing around to find the eggs.

"Marcus? Louise?" Mother said. "Here are your baskets. You're not going to let your sister find them all, are you?"

We each took a basket from her and looked at the woven straw and the bird's-nest filling of artificial grass. We glanced at each other. Half-heartedly, Marcus plucked a bright blue egg from the porcelain dish on the mantel and dropped it into his basket.

Then he said, "Stephie, do you want this blue one?"

She took it, placed it carefully in her basket with the others, and pranced off again.

"Is there more coffee, Hallie?" Father called from the kitchen.

"Coming," she called back and then turned to look at Marcus and me. "What's the matter?" she asked.

I set my empty basket down. "Uncle Claude hid something special for Marcus and me," I explained. "So we don't need the eggs. Stephie can have them."

"Where is Claude?" Marcus asked. "Isn't he up yet?"

"Hallie!" Father called again. "Is there any more coffee?"

She went to the kitchen. "Claude's gone," she called to Marcus and me. "He said he had to catch the early morning train."

"One, two, three, four, six." Stephie was counting her eggs with glee.

"You forgot five," I told her automatically. "One, two, three, four, *five*."

"*Gone?*" Marcus headed after Mother. I followed him. "What do you mean, Claude is gone?"

She poured more coffee into Father's cup. "Look

at this, you two," Father said, pointing proudly to the first page of the newspaper. "Now that is some photograph."

We looked dutifully at the large photograph reproduced on the page: a silhouette of a tree branch with a few tiny sprigs and buds; behind it, the sun was rising beyond the hills to the east of town. The caption said, "He is risen. He is risen indeed."

"Now normally," Father said, "I don't go for any religious connotations in headlines or captions. But I make an exception at Christmas and at Easter. The subscribers expect it."

"Yellow!" Stephie exclaimed. "I found a yellow one! One, two, three, four —"

"Why did he *leave*?" I asked Mother angrily. "Why didn't he tell us he was leaving? That's not fair! He hid something for us. What if we can't find it?"

Mother sighed and tucked a strand of loose hair back behind her ear. "You'll find it," she said. "You kids are the world's experts at finding things — that's why I always keep the Christmas presents at your father's office until Christmas Eve."

Marcus grinned. It was true. For years we had found and peeked at every Christmas present long before Christmas morning, until she had stopped trying to hide them at home.

"And as for why he left on the seven A.M. train — who knows? I thought he was leaving tonight. But when I got up this morning, he was gone.

Claude is completely unpredictable — you know that. He *did* leave you two a note, though. Matt, what did I do with that note that Claude left on the table?"

"Another green!" Stephie shouted happily.

Father looked up and glanced around as if he were searching for the note. "I don't know," he said and went back to the paper.

"Find it," I pleaded. "It might have clues."

Mother shuffled through the stack of papers on the table. "Let me think," she said. "He left one for me, too. It just said, 'Catching the Sunrise Express. Thanks for hospitality. Love, Claude.' I put mine with yours, and then I put them both —" She stood there with her head tilted, trying to remember.

"Here!" she announced triumphantly. "In my apron pocket." She reached in and took out two pieces of paper. One was open and crumpled, and the other neatly folded. She handed the folded one to me.

"Don't hog it, Louise," Marcus said, peering over my shoulder as I unfolded it. "It's for both of us."

"Right," I said. "It says at the top: 'Louisamanda and Marcus the Newbold.' "

Mother chuckled. "He always called himself 'Claude the Newbold' when he was a little boy," she said.

I read the note aloud. " 'I have other ports of call so must make a dawn retreet.' " I looked up at

Mother, a little embarrassed. "He spelled 'retreat' wrong," I said.

"That's not all it says," Marcus said impatiently. "Here. Let me read the rest." He grabbed the paper and went on. " 'They are well hidden. All treshures are well hidden, of course. Search hard, my comrades. Uncle Claude.' " He looked up and said petulantly, "There aren't any clues. And he spelled 'treasure' wrong, too."

"Wait," I said, and snatched the paper back. "There's something written on the bottom." The writing was tiny, and I squinted at it, but it was meaningless.

I pronounced the unintelligible words phonetically. "*Ya tebya lyublyu.*"

"Same to you," Marcus muttered. "Let me see it."

But when he read it aloud, it sounded the same. "*Ya tebya lyublyu.*"

"Let's try it backwards," I suggested. I took a pencil from the kitchen drawer and printed the words carefully in reverse. But it still meant nothing. *Uylbuyl aybet ay.* "You'll buy —" I started, but it made no sense after that.

Father looked up and chuckled. "You'll buy some worthless stock in a nonexistent oil well," he said. "That's what Claude tried to sell *me*, this time."

"Matt," Mother said, with a sigh, "you don't know for certain. It might actually have been worth something."

Father grinned. "I know he's your only brother, Hallie," he said, "but he's a con artist of the first order." He picked up the paper again.

But Marcus and I were barely listening to him. We were poring over the note, trying to decipher the words. It was obviously a code; and just as obviously, it related some hint to the whereabouts of the jeweled eggs.

"Is it French?" I asked Mother.

But she shook her head. "No."

"Swedish, maybe?"

"I don't know," she said. "But it doesn't sound like it. It doesn't sound like any language I've ever heard."

Stephie wandered into the room, her basket filled to the top with eggs, some of them cracked. "I'm hungry," she announced.

"I'll fix some breakfast for everyone," Mother said.

The front door opened and Tom came in, hanging his jacket in the hall on his way to the kitchen.

"Look!" said Stephanie to Tom. "Look at all my eggs!"

"Nice," he said to her, admiringly, and she smiled with satisfaction. Tom picked up the front section of the newspaper.

"Some picture on page one," he said to Father, who nodded, pleased, and turned back to the first page so that they could admire the photograph together.

"*Ya tebya lyublyu,*" I murmured to Marcus.

"*Ya tebya lyublyu,*" Marcus murmured back solemnly. Somewhere in our house was a hidden treasure; and somewhere, in the secret words, my brother and I held the key to it.

7

We searched. How we searched, Marcus and I! We started in my room, Easter morning, since it had been where Claude slept and would have been the obvious place to hide something.

There was no sign that Claude had been there at all. His suitcase was gone; the little box was gone; and he had even removed the blue sheets from my bed and put them into the laundry hamper in the bathroom.

"Think, Louise," Marcus commanded. "It's your room. Where would you hide something?"

I shrugged. "I always hide stuff under the bed," I said. "But we looked there. Or under my clothes, in the bureau, but we looked there."

"And we looked in the closet," Marcus said. "Even in all the shoes."

"*Ya tebya lyublyu,*" I repeated. "That first part sounds like 'the table.' Do you think it could mean 'the table' in some other language?"

"Maybe." We glanced around my room, but there were only two tables. The one beside my bed had only the small drawer where Claude had kept the Life Savers. We had looked in there. The other table, under a window, was where I did my homework. There were no hiding places in it.

I sighed. "It's not in this room," I said. "And it wouldn't be in the other bedrooms, because he hid it while everyone was asleep last night."

Marcus tested his ragged tooth with the tip of his tongue. "This house is full of tables," he pointed out. "Up in the attic and down in the basement and out in the shed — he could have gone there."

We looked through the window to the large, decrepit shed at the end of our driveway. Years ago, at the turn of the century, Mother said, a family probably had housed their cow or chickens there. They had stored wood there to heat the house in winter; now, of course, we had an oil furnace. Now the shed was dusty and cobwebbed and filled with junk. Marcus and I played in there, summers, fixing up forts and clubrooms, holding initiations, planning battles with the neighborhood kids. Each of us — even Tom — at some time or another, had been angered by some injustice and had run away, carrying a paper bag filled with food stolen from the refrigerator. We had ignored Mother's pleas to think twice, to be mature, to reach a compromise, and we had run away — always to the shed, where we had huddled miserably until evening came, shadows lengthened, the air grew cold, and we could hear mice scuttling and rustling. Then we would come home, trudging back along the driveway with tear-stained faces, to apologize and be welcomed back.

We would have to search the shed.

"Anyway," Marcus said, "it might not mean 'table.' *Ya tebya lyublyu*. That last word could mean 'blue.' He could have hidden it in something blue."

"A blue table," I suggested.

"We don't *have* a blue table."

I smoothed Claude's note and we looked at the words again. "Maybe," I said, "it's like those games in the children's page of the paper where you have to rearrange the letters?"

"I hate those," Marcus groaned.

"I do, too," I acknowledged. "But still: Look at the letters. Do you see any words?"

Marcus looked. "Bubbly," he said, finally.

"There aren't enough *b*'s," I decided.

"Yeah, but he can't spell, remember? Maybe he didn't know there are supposed to be three *b*'s in 'bubbly.'"

"*Great*," I said angrily. "It's bad enough to have to figure out a code. But when the guy who made the code can't spell? That's just *great*."

"Anyway," Marcus mused, "what would 'bubbly' mean?"

"Ginger ale," I suggested.

Marcus made a face. "No," he said. "That's dumb. I bet 'bubbly' would mean the river. Remember yesterday, how foamy and bubbly the river was? And Claude saw it, when we were over on the bank, behind the Leboffs' house."

"Well, now *you're* being dumb. How on earth could you hide something in the river? Anyway, he didn't want us to go back there. He said it was dangerous to prowl around the Leboffs' house, even outside."

We stared glumly at the note and finally I folded it up again and put it in the drawer of my little table.

"It has to be here at the house," Marcus said decisively. "You want to try the attic first or the shed?"

"The attic, I guess."

And so we went there.

"You two are absolutely filthy," Mother said when we came to dinner that evening. "What have you been doing? Look at your hands. Run up to the bathroom and *scrub*."

We did, and left the bathroom a disaster, with the towels streaked and the sink ringed with dirt.

"We were in the attic," I explained to Mother. "We were looking for Claude's gift."

"Oh?" She smiled. "And did you find it?"

"No," Marcus said dejectedly.

"I don't mind that he hid it," I told her. "But it's not fair that he hid it so we can't *find* it."

"Well," Mother said mildly, "that's Claude. He likes to complicate things. And remember what he said in his note? All treasures are well hidden."

She began to serve the food. Dinner on Easter was always the same: ham and deviled eggs, their whites stained with dye.

Father helped himself to salad and passed it around. "That's Claude all right," he echoed Mother. "But has it occurred to you two pipsqueaks that perhaps there was never any gift at all?"

Tom grinned, and popped half an egg into his mouth.

"Of course it occurred to us," I said. "We're not dumb. But you weren't there yesterday when Claude told us about it. He was absolutely sincere; wasn't he, Marcus?"

Marcus nodded, his mouth full.

"He was absolutely sincere when he tried to peddle a thousand dollars worth of fraudulent oil stock to me, too," Father said, grinning.

Tom swallowed his egg with a gulp and said, "He just makes stuff up. I think he's crazy."

"He teases, Tom," Mother said. "Claude is a tease, that's all."

I peeled a strip of fat carefully from a slice of ham and put it on the side of my plate. It fascinated me that some people — Marcus, for example —

could eat fat. I couldn't even stand the feel of it in my mouth. "Was he teasing when he said he'd been at the edge of the Baltic Sea?"

"It's hard to know, Louise," Mother said. "Claude drifts around so much — he's been to all sorts of places. I think it's quite likely that he's been to the edge of the Baltic Sea. Probably it was true."

"Could he have been to Russia, even?"

"It's possible. As he says, he's a traveling man. And once he did bring me an embroidered blouse — remember that, Matt? A beautiful blouse, made somewhere in Eastern Europe. Maybe Russia. It was before you were born, Louise."

That seemed to confirm Claude's veracity. He had brought the jeweled eggs out of Russia years ago, when it was still a Technicolor land, and had saved them, waiting for just the right people to give them to. He'd been waiting for us to be born.

"Well," I said with satisfaction, "then I'm quite sure he wasn't lying about the gift. I just wish he hadn't hidden it so well. Did he hide your blouse when he brought it to you?"

Mother laughed. "No. He had it in his suitcase, wrapped in newspaper, and he whipped it out with a big flourish. He was so delighted with it. I was, too, of course."

The telephone rang. Father pushed his chair back and went to the hall to answer it; we could hear his voice as he talked, and then he came back with his coat on.

"I have to go down to the office, Hallie," he said. "Save me some of that ham."

"Matt! It's almost seven o'clock on a Sunday night! Won't it wait till morning?"

Tom was up, out of his chair. "Can I go with you?"

"Do you have homework, Thomas?" Mother asked.

Tom shook his head. "It's all done. Can I go, Father?"

"Come on. Hurry. We have a big story breaking. There was a robbery last night; they've just discovered it. The police are still there."

He and Tom were at the front door. I was filled with excitement; there had never been robberies in our town. Our big news always consisted of flood damage, failed crops, rabid dogs, or an author or politician making a speech at the college.

I ran to the hall, opened the door, and called after them as they headed to the car.

"Where was it, Father? Did someone rob the bank?"

He turned, hesitated, and then shrugged. No harm in telling me, I could sense him thinking, since it would be in the morning paper anyway. He called out hurriedly where the robbery had been.

"Tell your mother not to wait up for me," he added. "I'll be late."

I gulped, waved half-heartedly to Father, went back to the table, and poked at the slick, glistening rims of fat on the edge of my plate. Mother and Marcus stared at me. Even Stephanie, in her high chair, looked at me curiously.

"Well?" Mother said after a moment. "What did Father say? We could hear you call to him from the front door."

Studiously I avoided looking at Marcus. Instead, I stared straight at Mother, my eyes as innocent as Stephie's. "Nothing much," I told her. "Someone robbed the Leboffs' house last night.

"What's for dessert?" I asked loudly. "I'm going to throw up if I eat any more Easter eggs."

8

Marcus and I cornered Kenny Stratton on the playground at recess. Kenny was an awkward, unpopular fifth-grader with a nervous twitch in one eyebrow, so that he lowered and raised it constantly, as if he were emphasizing the inane things he had to say. Marcus liked him, for some reason; he felt sorry for Kenny, whose mother had died years ago. The two Stratton children — Kenny and his older sister — kept house for their father in a shabby, two-family house at the edge of town. They both bragged about their father's association with the wealthy Leboff family; their bragging was undermined by the fact their clothes, hair, and hands were often in need of a good scrubbing.

Kenny had been boasting all morning, Marcus said, about his father's role in the discovery of the robbery at the Leboff's house. Mr. Stratton had made his usual six o'clock check of the mansion;

he had entered through the back door, using the key that hung in its hiding place. He had walked through the house, as he always did, checking the window locks. It was only when he got to the huge dining room that he felt something was wrong.

Kenny made a drama out of it again, telling it to Marcus and me one more time at the corner of the playground. He had told it so often this morning that he could build it now into a rehearsed tale, pausing for effect with his eyebrow jerking up and down like an undisciplined dancer.

"My father stood there in the dining room," Kenny said, "and he *knew* something was wrong." Pause. Twitch.

Kenny's eyes widened and he lowered his voice. "First he noticed that the big table — they call it the sideboard — was bare."

"It used to have all that silver stuff on it," Marcus said to me. "Remember?"

Kenny glared at him, irritated at the interruption. "The silver coffee service was gone," he went on. "So my dad started to open the drawers one by one." Pause.

"He messed up all the fingerprints, I bet," Marcus said, and Kenny glared at him again.

"And every bit of the silverware was gone. Two dozen knives, and two dozen forks, and two dozen spoons, and —"

Impatiently I interrupted him. "What did he do then? Did he call the police?"

"Of *course* he called the police," Kenny said. "For all he knew, the burglars might still have been there, hiding or something. He waited out by the back door — the police told him not to touch anything else — and they were there in seven minutes. My dad timed it."

We stood there silently, the three of us, under the maple tree at the corner of the playground. Nearby, our classmates were playing dodgeball, a cluster of them shrieking in the center of a circle while the ball thumped back and forth in pursuit. "You cheated, Charlie!" one of the girls shouted angrily, when she was hit on the leg.

"Poor sport, poor sport, poor sport," Charlie Clancy chanted as the outraged girl left the circle, rubbing her leg.

"What did the police do?" Marcus asked.

"They took inventory," Kenny said importantly, as if he knew what 'inventory' meant. "There was probably five thousand dollars worth of stuff taken."

"How did the burglars get in? Did they break a window or something?"

Kenny shook his head. "They found the key, where it was hidden. The police told my dad that the key should never have been left like that. But it wasn't my dad's fault. The Leboffs always left the key there. They *told* him to leave the key there." Kenny looked defensive on his father's behalf. "It wasn't my dad's fault," he said again.

I pictured Kenny's father, bald, skinny Mr. Stratton, sitting miserably in the police station, saying, "It wasn't my fault" again and again.

"Come around behind the tree," Marcus commanded; and we moved into the shadow, where the kids playing dodgeball couldn't see or hear us.

"Did your father know that we knew about the key? Did you tell him that we'd gone into the house?" Marcus asked.

Kenny's pinched, thin face looked more nervous than ever. He shook his head. "No," he whispered. "My dad doesn't even know that I've gone in there without him."

"Do you think our fingerprints are on the key?" Marcus asked tensely.

Kenny shook his head. "They said that my dad would have wrecked any fingerprints, because he was the last one to use the key when he went in to check the house. It wasn't his fault," he added again, absolving his father of yet one more mistake. "How was he supposed to know? The key was hanging right there the way it always did."

The bell rang, calling us back to class at the end of recess. We stood there for a moment, watching the other kids trudge reluctantly across the playground toward the school steps.

"They wanted a list from my father," Kenny added in a low voice as we began walking back. "The police wanted a list of everybody who knew about the key. But my father said he was the only one, except for Mrs. Shaw, and she's in Kansas City. They even called Kansas City long distance, and talked to Mrs. Shaw, and she said that nobody else knew about the key."

I kicked a stone across the muddy ruts of the playground. "Your father knew that you knew about it, Kenny," I pointed out.

"Yeah," Kenny acknowledged. "Because sometimes he takes me with him when he checks the house. But he didn't tell the police that. He said it wasn't important. He told me that he would have noticed if I'd come home with five thousand dollars worth of silver." He laughed morosely. "You better not tell, either," he added, "because then I'd tell on you."

Marcus and I shook our heads solemnly as a promise, and the three of us climbed the cement steps back into the school. "It wasn't my father's fault," Kenny said again in the empty hall as he and Marcus headed toward the fifth-grade room.

"Oh, shut up," I muttered, as I turned the corner to the door of the sixth grade. "Who cares?"

Usually I walked home from school with my friend Nancy Brinkerhoff, who lived a few houses away from mine. Marcus always dashed down the street with his friends, throwing their caps back and forth, calling insults to each other, making plans for ball games in the vacant lot.

But today Marcus and I walked home together.

At first we were silent. Then, suddenly, we both began talking almost at once.

"I don't care if Claude *did* know where the key was," I announced. "What does that prove? Probably *lots* of people knew where that key was. Kenny might have told other people."

"And Mrs. Shaw probably told her stupid daughter in Kansas City," Marcus said, "and her stupid daughter could have told *anybody*."

"And Claude doesn't need silverware, for heaven's sake," I said righteously. "He's a traveling man. A traveling man doesn't need silverware."

"Anyway," Marcus scoffed, "where would he have put it? All he had was that one dumb suitcase."

"And the box. You couldn't put five thousand dollars worth of silverware in that little bitty box." I shifted my schoolbooks to the other arm and tossed my head knowingly.

"Yeah," Marcus agreed. "Even if he *wanted* to steal all that stuff, where was he going to put it? In a pillowcase? He's going to walk to the train station carrying a pillowcase full of clanking silverware?"

We hooted with laugher at such a preposterous picture.

"*Ya tebya lyublyu*," I pronounced defiantly.

"*YA TEBYA LYUBLYU!*" Marcus shouted in response, with a grin.

We raced each other the rest of the way, reaching our front steps together and out of breath.

"Do you think maybe we ought to tell Mother?" I asked suddenly.

Marcus whirled around and stared at me. "That's a great idea, Louise," he said sarcastically. "Claude's her brother. What's she going to do? Call the police and tell them that her brother knew where the key was? Would you do that to *me* — even if you thought I was the thief, and we know Claude wasn't?"

"I never tell on you, Marcus. You know that."

"Yeah. So just shut up about it. I wish we knew where Claude went, so we could call him up and tell him what happened. Boy, would he laugh."

"He's probably a hundred miles away by now," I said.

"Probably a thousand."

"A *million*."

"Three million," Marcus decided. "He may be back in Russia by now, for all we know."

I walked backwards into the front yard, looking up, watching our house grow as I backed into a new perspective. The third story — the attic — seemed immensely high, and countless blank windows looked back at me. We had spent all of the previous afternoon in that attic, foraging in trunks and cubbyholes.

"Somewhere in there, Marcus." I sighed. "I know they're somewhere in that house, or in the shed. But it may take us *forever* to find them."

Marcus dropped his books on the porch and came to stand beside me. "You know something, Louise?

A house looks different, once it has a treasure inside. Even if we *never* find them, the house will always look different."

And he was right. I had always thought that our ordinary, shingled, unglamorous house was much like every other house on the block. It was no more interesting than Nancy Brinkerhoff's; we had a porch swing and the Brinkerhoffs didn't, but they had a chiming doorbell and ours was only a dull buzz. Even Mrs. Bostwick's house was ordinary, now that she had died and it had been sold to a young lawyer and his wife; they had painted and repaired it, planted flowers in the once unkempt yard, and to-day their baby's playpen stood on the porch, the way Stephie's had always stood on ours until she out-grew it. Ours had always been an ordinary street of ordinary houses filled with ordinary things and people.

Until now. Now our house was special, because Claude had come and gone, and now, somewhere, we had a treasure.

9

"Hey, Lulu," Tom called from his room. "Come in here a minute, will you?"

"The name is Louise," I said automatically, and folded the piece of paper on which I had been rearranging the letters of Claude's mysterious message. I put it into the drawer of my bedside table and went to the hall. Tom was standing in the doorway of his bedroom.

"What do you want?" I asked him.

"I want to talk to you. Marcus, too. Where is he?"

"He's in the attic. I'll call him." I went to the attic stairs and summoned Marcus, who shook his head at me as he came down, streaked once again with dirt. Nothing. He had found nothing.

We went to Tom's room, and I marveled once again, as I always did, how someone fourteen years old could be so tidy and organized. Mother was not as good a housekeeper as Tom. His books were arranged alphabetically, and if you borrowed one without asking and put it back in the wrong spot, he knew; and you were *dead*. His clothes were always hung up; his bed was always made; and even his baseball cap was on a shelf and his sneakers were lined up neatly side by side below it.

Marcus and I sat down on Tom's bed, and Tom sat at his desk, facing us, the way I imagined that a doctor would when he told you that you were going to die soon. And Tom had that same look on his face, the look that the doctor would have: grave, no-nonsense, and very concerned.

"I have a stone in my shoe," I announced, "and it's been there all day. I bet anything I'm going to have foot gangrene." Changing the subject was the way I handled anything that made me feel apprehensive, and Tom's look was making me feel apprehensive.

"If you do," Marcus said, "they'll have to cut your foot off. But they can make pretty good artificial ones."

"Listen, you two," Tom said, ignoring my foot gangrene, "I was talking to Joyce Stratton at school today."

I leaned over to investigate the stone in my shoe more thoroughly. Joyce Stratton was Kenny's older sister, and she was just as skinny and boring as Kenny, but I sure wished that Tom hadn't been talking to her.

"So?" Marcus said.

"So. She said that Kenny knew about that key, and that he had shown it to you kids, and that all three of you had been in the Leboffs' house."

"So, you know what that proves, Thomas Frederick Cunningham? It proves that Joyce Stratton knew about it, too! And maybe she was the person who robbed the house!" I drew myself up, prepared to testify against Joyce Stratton till the end of time.

"Yeah," Marcus added. "Joyce Stratton hangs around with that whole gang of junior high girls, and maybe they all did it together. Heck, maybe you even did it with them, Tom!"

Tom leaned back in his chair with a patient sigh. "Look, pip-squeaks," he began.

I interrupted him angrily. "Don't you dare call us that! Only Father calls us that!"

Tom tried again. "Okay, I'm sorry. But look, you guys. I know you didn't steal the stuff. And Joyce and Kenny didn't steal the stuff. I'm only trying to tell you that you could have gotten yourselves into a lot of trouble, breaking into the Leboffs' house —"

"It wasn't breaking into," Marcus said. "When you have a key, it isn't breaking into."

"Listen to me, will you? I'm trying to tell you that you should *think* before you do stuff like that. Think about what could happen if you got caught. I don't want you dragging the name of this family through the mud."

I giggled, picturing the letters that spelled Cunningham, at the end of a string, being dragged down the street through puddles and dirt. Tom glared at me.

"Are you going to tell on us?" Marcus asked.

"Of course I'm not. I just wanted to have a talk with you, that's all."

"You can't tell us what to do, Tom," I said belligerently. "You're not Father. And you're only fourteen."

"I know that. And I've done a lot of stupid stuff, too. But I don't go around breaking into people's houses." Tom stood up. "Well, anyway, I just wanted to warn you. If you end up in jail, don't say I didn't warn you."

Dismissed, Marcus and I left Tom's room and went to mine, where we closed the door, fell onto my bed, and laughed. "He never even guessed that Claude knew, too!" I said with pleasure.

Marcus imitated Tom's serious voice: "I don't want you dragging the name of this family —"

"THROUGH THE MUD!" I shrieked and fell over again, laughing.

"You know what Tom is?" Marcus whispered.

"What?"

He lowered his voice even more, until I could barely hear him. "A turd," he said with furtive glee.

I pounded my fists on the bed with delight. We repeated the wonderful, forbidden word over and over again, roaring with laughter until our stomachs ached, muffling our mouths with the pillows from my bed, until Mother called to tell us that Father was home and it was time to wash our hands for dinner.

In the evening, I did my homework half-heartedly, sitting at the table under my bedroom window. Outside, it was beginning to rain: first a light spring drizzle, then increasing in force until it pelted the house fiercely. Mother came upstairs to check the windows.

"Did you put your bike in the shed?" she asked Tom.

"Of course. I always put my bike away."

I could hear Marcus puttering in his room next to mine. "'Of course,'" I heard him mimic Tom in a low, exaggerated voice, "'I *always* put my bike away.'"

"Well," Mother said, sticking her head into my doorway, "I left the sheets on the clothesline. I guess there's no point in going out to get them now."

"If it's still pouring in the morning, do you think Father will give us a ride to school?" I asked her.

"I suppose so," she said. "The radio says it isn't going to let up. I hope it doesn't ruin the forsythia." She came over to my window and looked out, but the bright forsythia bush beside the driveway was invisible through the driving rainstorm.

"Mother," I asked, pushing my geography book aside. I unfolded Claude's note again. "Do you think it's true that Claude is crazy, like Tom said?"

She sighed. "Oh, Louise, who knows what 'crazy' means? He's *different*, certainly. He always has been."

"What was he like when he was a kid?"

She sat down on my bed. "Well, he was different then, too. He's the only child I've ever known who created whole worlds for himself. He always had entire cities built out of blocks — or later, when he was older, out of Erector sets — in his room."

"All kids do that. Marcus does."

"Yes, but — well, this was different. His cities and worlds became very real to him. Sometimes it was as if he lived in those worlds, instead of the real one."

"I don't understand what you mean."

"Once, out in our back yard, he built a tree house. It was the most wonderful tree house, with little windows and a ladder that he could pull up after he was inside so that no one else could climb it. Sometimes he slept out there."

"Did he let you play in it? Or was he selfish, like Marcus?"

She smiled. "Marcus isn't selfish, Louise. He's just a normal boy. Claude was a lot like Marcus in some ways: cheerful and fun. He always had wonderful ideas, but sometimes they were so complicated, and sometimes he took them so seriously, that the other kids in our neighborhood would get sick of him, and they'd go off to play their own games."

"What do you mean?"

"Well, the tree house, for example. After it was

built — and he took a long time to build it, and wouldn't let anyone help — he did invite a group of neighborhood children to climb up. And me, too. It was the first time I'd been in his tree house. We were all thrilled, of course, because it was truly the most spectacular tree house we'd ever seen. But then Claude started explaining the *rules* of the tree-house —"

"That's okay. I can understand about having rules, especially if you built it all by yourself."

"Yes, but Claude had created one of his worlds up there in that tree. He had made it into a kingdom — I remember he even called it that: kingdom. He was the king, of course."

"That's fair," I said. I could sympathize with that, the need to be king if you had invented the kingdom.

"But more than that. He had made up a language, and we were to speak only that language when we were in the tree house kingdom. And there was a set of complicated laws. Rules about the kind of food you could eat and particular sorts of clothes that people in the kingdom were to wear. I seem to remember that he had even created a special religion for this kingdom, with songs and prayers, all in this strange language that he had spent hours concocting."

"I think that's a great idea!"

She smiled. "It would have been. But Claude took it all so seriously. It was one of his fantasies that grew out of proportion, so that it became too real, at least to him. The kids got bored. The language was too complicated, and he said we couldn't come into the tree house until we learned it. Everybody just gave up."

"Even you?"

"Well, I stuck with it longer than the others. So for a while, it was just he and I in the tree house, speaking this odd language to each other. But after a while, I got bored with it, too. For me it was a game, I guess. And for Claude it really was a whole world; it seemed quite real to him, and important, and he forgot that it was all just a pretend thing. I think he kept it up for a year or so, all by himself. He was about Marcus's age, then."

Something occurred to me. "Do you remember any of the language?"

She shook her head.

I pulled out the sheet of notebook paper that I had been writing on and showed it to her.

L

YA

U

TEBYA

L

Y

U

"I'm still trying to figure this out," I explained. "Could it be from his tree house language?"

"I don't think so, Louise," Mother said, examining the words. "I don't remember the language, but I remember the sound of it. It wasn't like this."

"Well," I sighed, "I keep rearranging it, but it doesn't make any sense."

She smiled. "You know what your father would say? That Claude himself doesn't make any sense. And maybe that's true. But you know, Louise, there was always something very special about Claude. It's hard to explain. Often the other kids called him a liar, especially when he insisted that his made-up world was real. But I never thought that his fantasies were lies — they were more a magical kind of thing. When you're with Claude — and this was true even when we were children — the most everyday things seem, well, charmed."

Charmed. I liked her choice of words. It was true.

"I wonder where he is now," she said suddenly, and went to the window again, to peer through the torrents of rain that were slapping the side of our house now in punishing sheets. "He takes off like that, with no idea where he's going, heading for the most obscure places, just —" She shrugged.

I finished the sentence for her. "Just passing through."

She laughed. "Finish your homework, Louise," she said. "It's almost nine o'clock."

When she had gone, Marcus came into my room, grinning. "I have a surprise," he said. "I've been working on it ever since supper."

"You were supposed to be doing your homework," I told him, feeling as I said it that I sounded like Tom.

"Sit on your bed," he said, and pointed to the exact spot where he wanted me. "And wait. I'm almost through. Just wait there and see what happens!"

Obediently I sat where he had told me to. He went back to his room, and I waited. I could hear small scraping noises from Marcus's side of the wall. They continued: rhythmic, digging sounds, through the sound of the rain outside, almost the same sounds we could hear occasionally in the shed when mice scurried and gnawed invisibly behind the old planks and boards.

"What are you *doing*?" I called impatiently.

The noise stopped, and Marcus appeared again in my doorway. "Watch your wall," he ordered in a loud and self-important whisper.

I sighed. I hated it when Marcus ordered me around; after all, I was a year older than he. I thought of Mother, a year older than Claude, being ordered to learn a language and a set of laws for an imaginary kingdom. And I sat there on my bed, dutifully watching the wall, because whatever Marcus was up to, it was bound to be fun.

A small flower on my wallpaper, slightly above the table beside my bed, began to shiver and move. I stared in amazement. Seconds later, a yellow petal on the flower disappeared. I blinked. Where the petal had been, a shiny piece of metal appeared, and then grew larger. A tiny puff of plaster dust poofed into the air and fell to the table. With a final shove, the end of a screwdriver emerged into my room through the wall; it moved briefly in a rotating pattern and was withdrawn. I could hear Marcus's breath as he blew through the hole, and more plaster dust flew out and settled on the table.

I leaned over to look more closely. I could see the light from Marcus's room. Then the hole darkened; I could hear a rustling sound, and an instant later, something new began to appear in the hole. I reached for it and drew it through: a piece of paper rolled tightly into a cylinder.

I unrolled it and read: HELLO FROM MARCUS THE NEWBOLD.

I took it to my desk, found my pencil, and wrote: LOUISAMANDA SENDS GREETINGS. MOTHER IS GOING TO KILL YOU WHEN SHE FINDS OUT.

ARE YOU GOING TO TELL? Marcus sent back.

I marched to his room and found him hunched over his side of the hole.

"No," I assured him. "I'm not going to tell."

Later, when I was in bed, and Mother had checked the windows one more time, and outside the rain was still a heavy deluge against the roof and sides of the house, I heard the rustling sound again, near my head. I reached toward the wall and felt the rolled paper appear. I turned on the light, and read:

JUST PASSING THROUGH.

10

It rained and rained. Mother's sheets flapped in the wet wind for days until finally she dashed outside with a raincoat draped over her head, took them down, rewashed them, and hung them in the basement in disgust.

The forsythia blossoms were all gone by the first day, pulled loose from the fragile stems, smashed to the ground beside the driveway, and then washed away in the water that had changed from puddles to rivulets to torrents that streamed from the drive-way into the wet street.

The after-school softball games were a thing of the past, now that the vacant lot where they had been played had become a brown sea in which Popsicle wrappers drifted and churned. Tom stayed in his room in the afternoons, working on a school project; Stephie, bored with her indoor toys, whined and made a pest of herself. One afternoon I held her against the window and pointed to her sandbox, showing her that it was awash in the ocean that had once been our back yard.

"It's a boat now, Stephie," I told her. But she wailed, following her favorite tin shovel with her eyes as it moved in aimless circles through the water. She kicked me angrily, pushed herself out of my arms, and ran to cling to Mother's skirt.

School continued, with recess held indoors now. The distracted teachers dreamed up activities we could do at our desks: word games and art projects. But we misbehaved, making paper airplanes with our construction paper, calling loudly across the room to special friends, all of us outraged that our outdoor world had spurned us and was keeping us prisoners here in a chalk-smelling room.

Many school desks were empty. The buses still came in every morning from the country, but only the girls from the farms came to school. Their brothers were kept at home to help try to save their land, for the interminable driving rain was pulverizing the rich topsoil and washing it away, and the mud-filled river was rising and threatening the fields. In my sixth-grade class, the Sorenson twins, Anders and Karl, were absent; and sturdy Nicholas Rostov was gone, though his sister Lydia still came every day to third grade, running from the bus with her kerchief tightly knotted under her chin and rain streaks on her ruddy face.

Father was tense and agitated in the evenings and was frequently on the telephone. The robbery at the

Leboffs' house, though still unsolved, was old news now; there were more immediate concerns. The river was higher already than it had been in years, the rain was still coming down, and if it didn't stop, there would be a flood.

Yet in other parts of the country, there was sunshine. Marcus and I knew because Claude sent us a postcard to tell us so. Claude was apparently in Denver, far to our west.

"In Denver the sun is shining," I told Mother, holding the treasured postcard.

"Actually," I went on, looking at the card again, "the sun is *shinning* in Denver. At least that's what he says."

It still bothered me that Claude — a man who'd been to the edge of the Baltic Sea — couldn't spell. "Well," the postcard addressed to me and Marcus read, "hear I am in Denver, Colaraddo, would you beleive it? The sun is shinning."

I didn't want Father or Tom to know and to ridicule Claude. But privately I showed the card to Mother and watched her face as she read it. She simply smiled and gave it back to me.

"He must have been in a hurry when he wrote it," I suggested. "See how he spelled things wrong? Same as the note he left for us. And I know he was in a hurry then, to catch the train."

But she said no. "That's just Claude," she said. "Such a talker — he always was, even as a child. But reading and writing came hard for Claude. He was never much for school."

I told Marcus what she had said, and he rubbed his tongue across his jagged-edged tooth and nodded. "Like you and diving," he pointed out matter-of-factly.

I glared at him for a moment. But he wasn't needling me, not this time; he was simply stating a fact. And it was a fact. I was an excellent swimmer, "a veritable fish," Father always said proudly. Every summer we spent a month in a rented cottage on the shore of the small lake fifteen miles east of town. I had learned to swim there so long ago that I could no longer remember the learning. The water was like air to me; I felt at home in it, and every morning, even when it rained, I ran across the tiny pebbled beach and, without pausing, continued into the lake until I was submerged. Then I would simply go on, running merging naturally into swimming, and I moved easily, weightless and supple, through the cold green fluid world. I never tired. Sometimes for hours I propelled myself through the lake, under the water or on its surface, occasionally so far out that I could look back toward shore and see the cottage and my family on the beach, flattened in perspective like cardboard scenery on a stage. From the distance I could hear Mother's voice: "Not so far, Louise!" and I would knife my way back, slicing through the water, to placate her, peering through my beaded, watery eyelashes until she waved and smiled, reassured.

I was as buoyant and facile in the lake as Claude was with speech. But I couldn't dive. Tom was an agile, competent diver who had won awards at Boy Scout camp. And even Marcus, a thrashing dog-paddler easily given to panic if he couldn't feel the stony bottom under his feet, could fling himself fearlessly, headfirst, from the splintery dock. He could do it forward, backward, curled into a ball, or with his arms spread wide.

"It's easy, Louise!" Tom and Marcus would tell me every summer. Yet when I stood on the edge of the dock looking down into the lake, the water seemed to change. It was murky, dark, and terrifying from that unaccustomed angle; and when finally, shivering, I would force my legs to move like springs and send me into the air and down, I would fall awkwardly, slapping my stomach, stinging my knees, and I would come to the surface choking, angry, and humiliated.

I turned Claude's misspelled postcard over in my hands, and wondered if Marcus was right, if Claude felt that way, scared and incompetent, when he held a pen and tried to plunge into something that came so naturally to the rest of us.

After we had examined it carefully for new messages or clues — but there were none; there was only that foolish, misspelled greeting — Marcus and I tucked the card away in the drawer of my bedside table with Claude's note. It was reassuring, at least, to know that he was still thinking of us. Surely one day soon he would write to ask if we had found his gift; he would give us an address, and we could write to him and ask humbly for his help. We still searched diligently, almost every day. But we were running out of places to look.

And now, when we searched in the basement, our shoes got wet. The water had seeped up through the cement floor, in uneven lines where the floor was cracked, and soon it had spread a damp film across the entire surface. Father checked the furnace every day before he went to his office.

One evening he came home from work dripping, as usual. He spread his wet coat over the staircase railing to dry, peeled off his boots in the kitchen, and poured himself a drink.

He turned to us and went through his usual routine, though it was wearing thin by now. "Raining cats and dogs, right, pip-squeaks?" he asked.

"Better than hailing taxicabs," Marcus and I responded as we had now for days, and he ran his hands through our hair and smiled. But his thoughts were obviously elsewhere.

"I have to go back in to the office after dinner, Hallie," he said to Mother. "The National Guard's coming in tonight with sandbags. The wall's crumbling along the west edge of the cemetery. And up along the River Road, Peter Marek's whole pasture is under water. His cows are all in the barn, but if the water gets higher it'll cut the barn off, too. They're going to try to move his whole herd across the road to Anderson's land later this evening."

Mother shook her head and began to put dinner on the table.

"Alexandra Marek's in my class at school," I said. "I bet she gets to stay up and watch. I never get to watch anything interesting."

Father chuckled. "You and Marcus can watch our furnace," he told us. "If the water comes up around the base of the furnace, I want you to push that red switch that says 'Off' at the top of the basement stairs. Promise?"

"All right," I said grudgingly. "But I'd rather be out there watching them herd cows through a flood."

"I'd rather see the wall of the cemetery falling apart," Marcus said. "Then all the dead bodies will start falling into the river." He made a ghoulish face and was about to go into his vampire imitation, but Mother stopped him.

Tom came from his room and sat down at the table. Mother lifted Stephanie into her high chair and began to serve dinner.

"Is it true?" Tom asked. "Is the cemetery wall going?"

Father nodded. "They're going to sandbag it," he said.

"Can I go? Can I help them?"

But this time Father said no. "You're too young, Tom, and it's too dangerous. The river hasn't been this bad in my lifetime. Somebody's going to get killed before this ends."

"You won't be in danger, will you, Matt?" Mother asked with a worried frown.

He smiled. "I almost wish I could say yes. I wish

I could help them. But I'll be in my office, high and dry. You can call me there if you need me."

"High and dry," Stephie said, grinning. "High and dry." She reached for a drumstick.

11

In the morning Father wasn't at the breakfast table. Usually he was there, freshly shaved and checking for errors in the paper; lately, with the weather as an excuse, we had wheedled him each day into driving us to school. But today he was still in bed.

"He's exhausted," Mother explained. "He didn't get in until three this morning."

"Did the National Guard come? Did they sandbag the cemetery wall?" Marcus asked.

"Did they move the Mareks' cows?" I wanted to know. Alexandra Marek was going to be the center of attention in school today, I speculated enviously. Her family's farm was the closest to the river; they were the first real victims. And Alexandra was a show-off, given to drama; I knew she would be telling a tale of danger and terror, embellishing it all day with new details.

"Take a look," Mother replied, and handed me the paper. There, on the front page, was a picture of frightened cows being herded across a road that itself looked like a river. Then I looked further, and groaned with jealousy; there was another, smaller picture, of Alexandra herself, wrapped in a blanket, being carried by a strange man through knee-deep water.

"Read the article," Mother said. "They moved the whole Marek family out. The water's up to the first floor of their house."

"I don't need to read it," I said, sulking, and set the paper aside. "I'll be hearing about it all day in school."

"What about the cemetery?" Marcus asked, with his mouth full of toast.

"There's an article about that, too," Mother told him. "They gave up on the cemetery because there are so many houses threatened down in the lower end of town. So they're sandbagging down there — they have been all night, I guess. They had to let the cemetery go. Your father said that the wall caved in entirely, in the middle of the night."

"Are bodies floating out?" Marcus asked, his eyes wide.

Mother wiped Stephanie's egg-smeared face with a damp cloth. "Of course not," she said matter-of-factly. "That side of the cemetery is almost a hundred years old. Anyone who was buried there that long ago would have decomposed and become part of the earth by now. Don't fill your sister's head with wild nonsensical ideas." She lifted Stephie out of her high chair, and my sister padded away in her pajamas with flannel feet attached.

Marcus whispered to me in the hall as we pulled on our rubber boots and slickers. "There would still be bones," he said. "I bet anything that leg bones and arm bones are floating out. Wouldn't it be neat to see that?"

I simply made a face. The macabre specter of old bones sliding out of the earth into the river didn't interest me at all. I was much more concerned about the fact that Alexandra Marek had had her picture on the front page of the paper, and I never had.

We called good-by to Mother and headed out into the pelting rain.

To my relief, Alexandra wasn't in school. Many more children were absent today than previously; there were only fourteen kids in my class, and Mrs. Higgins cancelled the spelling test she had planned. Instead, she announced, we would spend the day studying flood-related things. In geography, we would learn about the Nile Delta and how its floods each year enriched the earth (which puzzled me, since *our* flood was washing our farmlands away); for science, we would turn to the chapter about weather; and for current events, we would each stand and tell about how our families were affected by this catastrophic rain.

Great, I thought, gloomily. Looking around the room, I could see that there were kids present whose homes were in that low, threatened part of town by the river. They would have wild stories to tell, I was quite sure. And I? I made up my report in my head:

"My sister's sandbox turned into a boat and floated over against the side of our shed. There is about one inch of water in our basement, and if it goes up to a foot deep we have to turn the red furnace switch to 'off.' And my mother's forsythia bush had all its blossoms washed away."

Well, at least I could tell about my father, and that he didn't get home until three A.M. He had been in charge, there at the newspaper office; it had been he who courageously sent his photographer out in the middle of the night to take pictures of —

I glowered. Pictures of Alexandra Marek, heroine of the flood. Carried in the arms of a dashing stranger through the swirling water.

Couldn't she have *walked*, for heaven's sake? The water was only up to the guy's knees, and Alexandra was tall for a sixth-grader. Her desk was in front of mine, and during filmstrips I always had to lean sideways to see around her because her shoulders and head stuck up so high.

Gloomily I stared out the window at the rain and half-listened to Mrs. Higgins's voice droning on.

Then, in the middle of geography, there was an announcement. School was closing. It was only ten in the morning, but we were all to go home. A cheer went up in our classroom, and even Mrs. Higgins looked relieved.

"Bus people first," she said, and five children rose from their desks and went to the coatroom to struggle back into their raincoats and boots.

"And no homework tonight," Mrs. Higgins announced. Gleefully we put our books into our desks.

When the bus people had filed out, the rest of us were released. Leaving the school building, I looked around and realized how much we all looked alike today; we were a uniformed army of bright yellow slickers. With the waterproof hats that framed our faces and hid our hair, it was hard to tell who was who.

I recognized Marcus when he left his group of look-alike fifth-graders and came over to me. The windy rain carried away his voice and I couldn't hear what he was saying. "What?" I shouted; and we both turned so that the wind was at our backs.

"Mother won't know that school was let out, so we don't have to go home right away," he repeated.

"Mrs. Higgins said we were all to go right straight home."

"'Mrs. Higgins said we were all to go right straight home,'" Marcus mimicked in a high voice.

"Quit it," I said.

"You want to come with me?"

"Where?" I asked. "Where are you going?"

"Just down to the cemetery. I want to see if the bones are floating out."

"You are *not*. Father said we were absolutely not to go anywhere near the river. Anyway, who wants to see disgusting bones?"

"Me. I do. You coming?"

"No."

He hesitated. I looked around. All of the other children had straggled off; some of them were jumping in the deep puddles at the corner, but most had walked, hunched over in the rain, directly down the street and toward their homes.

"Are you going to tell on me?" Marcus asked. His eyes were scrunched up and there were raindrops dripping from his chin.

It was such a familiar question, and there was only one answer to it; we both knew that. Of course I wouldn't tell. I sighed.

"Tell you what, Marcus," I said, finally. "It's a quarter past ten. I'll go over to the library and wait there for you. But if you're not there in half an hour, I'm going home. And then Mother will know, whether I tell or not."

"Okay." Marcus turned and was gone — not running, because it was almost impossible to run against the wind — but walking fast, bent over to keep the rain out of his eyes, heading for the cemetery. I turned in the other direction and sloshed through the puddles half a block to the public library. By the time I reached its steps, I was drenched, despite my slicker. The warmth and light inside were welcoming.

"My goodness," Mr. Mueller, the librarian, said, looking up from his desk, "Louise Cunningham. You're my only customer today. Why aren't you in school?"

I lifted my yellow helmet and wiped my wet face with one hand. "They closed the school," I told him. "So I thought I'd just stop by and find a book for a book report, before I go home."

He reached into a drawer of his desk and handed me a paper towel. "Here," he said. "Wipe your hands and face. Maybe you ought to take off your wet coat, too."

I did, and hung it on the coatrack in the corner. Then I wandered, my wet shoes squishing inside my boots, into the children's room.

"Are you looking for anything special, Louise?" Mr. Mueller called. "Do you want some help?"

"No, thank you," I called back.

Then I thought of something. I went back to his desk, where he was busily typing something on index cards.

"Do you have any books about Russia?" I asked.

"Of course. Do you want Travel, or History, or Political Systems, or Language?"

"I don't know." It hadn't occurred to me that there would be so many different aspects of Russia and that there would be books for each.

"Well, what is it you want to know about Russia? Are you studying it in school?" Mr. Mueller looked genuinely interested. I had always liked him; he was chubby and cheerful, but usually there were lots of people in the library, and he never had time for conversation.

"No. But someone was telling me—well, you may not know anything about this, Mr. Mueller, but someone was telling me that in Russia they used to have these fabulous Easter eggs. Not regular Easter eggs, but ones with real jewels on them, like diamonds and stuff."

To my surprise, he was nodding. "Oh, yes," he said, "the Fabergé eggs."

So they were real, and not part of an imaginary world dreamed up by Uncle Claude. I hadn't said so to Marcus, but after our days of fruitless searching, and after hearing Mother tell about Claude's tree house kingdom, I had entertained vague doubts about the eggs. But Mr. Mueller — who knew everything there was to know about everything — was nodding vigorously and with interest.

He stroked his chin. "I wonder," he said, "whether it would be best to look under Jewels, or Art Treasures, or whether maybe there might be a listing under . . ."

His voice drifted off, and he went to the card catalogue. I looked at the big clock on the wall. Twenty minutes had passed since I left Marcus.

The library was silent except for the rustle of Mr. Mueller sorting cards to look at them. He closed one drawer and opened another.

"I just thought I'd check first to see if there was perhaps a listing under Fabergé," he explained. "He was the man who created the eggs. No one has ever been able to duplicate them.

"But there's nothing listed under his name. Now, let me think. I believe I'll try Jewels, though I doubt . . ." He opened another drawer and moved his fingers through the cards.

I shifted my weight in my wet boots and glanced again at the clock. Twenty-four minutes had gone by.

"I should *know* this," Mr. Mueller said apologetically. "After all, I'm the one who catalogues these books. But you know, Louise, I've been here seventeen years. And one does forget things after seventeen years. A *few* things, anyway." He chuckled. He opened another drawer. "I think I'll look under Art. It's easier, you know, when something is clearly defined. Now if you'd asked me about Rembrandt, of course, I would look under Art. But those eggs: Well, that's an odd category. No question that they were works of art, but . . ."

He leaned over and shuffled through the cards in the drawer marked *A*. I could hear the clock tick in the silence. I willed myself not to look at it again right away.

The *A* drawer snapped closed. Mr. Mueller's chubby face was red with frustration. "You know," he mused, stroking his chin again, "I just might try Kremlin. I seem to remember that those eggs are stored in the museum in the Kremlin. In seventeen years you are the first person who has ever asked me this particular question, Louise; isn't that amazing?"

I broke my vow and looked at the clock. Thirty minutes exactly. I went to the door of the library and listened for the sound of Marcus on the steps, but the only sound was the sound of rain. I took my slicker from the coatrack and put it on. Mr. Mueller was still at the card catalogue, muttering.

"Mr. Mueller," I said politely, "I have to go."

He looked up in dismay. "You do? But—"

"I'll come back. And in the meantime, maybe you will have figured out where to find it. But I have to go now. I promised somebody."

"You know what I'll do, Louise? I'll look through the big art books. I'm quite sure that I'll locate it in one of those. And come to think of it, I seem to remember that there was a magazine article once. I'll get out my *Readers' Guide to Periodical Literature*, and—"

"Thanks, Mr. Mueller." I looked at the clock again. Marcus had been gone now for thirty-five minutes. He had a watch. He would know how much time had passed. I felt, suddenly, very frightened. "I really have to go now."

I pulled the door open, let myself out, and adjusted my hat in the blinding rain. There was no sign of Marcus. Fighting the wind, I began to run in my heavy, wet boots toward the cemetery.

12

I had only four blocks to go to reach the edge of the cemetery. But my feet were heavy, the wind was against me, trying to push me backward, and it was hard to see. The visor of my slicker helmet kept slipping down over my forehead and I pushed it up automatically as I ran. At the corner, the water was so deep across the street that I couldn't see the curb, and I slipped and fell. My boots filled with the ice-cold, muddy water, and I had to stop on the other side of the street and empty them as best I could.

I ran on, past the deserted school; the playground was covered with brown water and the swings moved in the wind and clanked against their metal supports.

There were no cars on the streets, no people, no dogs, nothing of the everyday life of our town. But suddenly I became aware of a new sound, a swishing through the water, and a presence nearby. I tilted my visor, looked up, and saw a bicycle with a drenched figure on it. Startled, I realized it was my brother, Tom.

"Louise!" he yelled angrily. "What the *hell* are you doing? And where's Marcus? Mother sent me out to find you. They closed all the schools almost an hour ago!"

I tried to sound casual, though I had a sharp pain in my side from running and was still gripped with a feeling of fear for Marcus. But I shrugged with pretended nonchalance, my shoulders lifting inside my slicker.

"I went to the library. And stupid Marcus went down to the cemetery to see if any bones were floating out. I'm just going to meet him, and then we'll be right home. Tell Mother we'll be there in a few minutes, okay?"

He didn't answer, but he looked furious, and I didn't blame him. I would have been furious, too. In fact, suddenly I was terribly angry at Marcus. If it weren't for him, I would have been home drinking hot chocolate at this very minute, instead of being dripping wet and freezing cold.

Tom sprayed me with more cold water from the wheels of his bike when he rode off toward home without looking back. I realized that it was the first time I had ever heard him swear. Maybe, I thought with satisfaction, I would tell on him when I got home, and he would be in trouble along with Marcus and me.

Where *was* Marcus? I was nearing the cemetery now, after struggling along for the remaining blocks, and there was still no sign of him. I hated the cemetery. Mother had tried to point out to me how pretty it was, planted with flowers and bushes everywhere; some people even had picnics there in summer. But to me it was just a place where dead people were. Our old neighbor, Mrs. Bostwick, was in there somewhere, and so was Mrs. Mallory's husband, the one who had died of the mysterious fever long ago. Kenny Stratton's mother was there in the cemetery, too. The place gave me the creeps, and I always crossed the street to the other side when I had to walk past its low stone wall.

Now I had to enter it, and I would never *ever* forgive Marcus for that. The flowers and bushes, like Mother's forsythia, were battered and smashed by the rain. The gravestones, still standing in the blanket of water, tilted crazily. Here and there, higher places were still exposed, but it seemed eerie, seeing those rounded hills like the naked shoulders of a floating corpse.

"Marcus!" I yelled, standing ankle-deep in the path. But there was no answer, and I knew that if he was — as I expected — still down at the river's edge, he couldn't possibly hear me.

I sloshed on, and the noise of the water under my feet and slicing down through the trees from the sky was now intensified by the rushing sound of the river. Ordinarily this was such a quiet place. But today, as I approached the oldest section of the cemetery, the area that bordered the river, it roared with the sound of water. My voice — though I continued calling Marcus's name — was lost, washed away by the violent raging turmoil I could hear ahead.

Now, suddenly, I could see what once had been the wall that divided the river from the land. Crumbling, Father had said. But it hadn't crumbled; it had heaved and smashed; it had been blasted by the fury of the flood, and I could see the huge rocks of the wall being lifted by the water's brown, surging force, pounded against each other and tossed like pebbles in the foaming waves. Behind the demolished wall, in the cemetery itself, the water was moving and the gravestones, too, were being uprooted and tumbled about like toys.

And now, at last, I could see Marcus. His brilliant yellow slicker stood out against the brown and gray muddled, writhing mixture of land and water.

"Damn you, Marcus!" I shouted, overwhelmed by anger as Tom had been. "Damn you, damn you!" I had fought my way through this storm to find him, and now I would face Mother's wrath, and Tom's and Father's, and here he was; he had forgotten his promise to meet me, and he was standing there like a ghoulish idiot, looking for bones.

He hadn't seen me yet, and no wonder: The river was surging immediately in front of him, waves breaking and crashing over the rocks at the base of the demolished wall; the water was swirling right over his feet and up to his knees. The idiot! Why didn't he move back! But he wasn't even looking at the angry water. He was looking up and to the side, and I followed the direction of his eyes and saw that a large tree had been torn practically in half by the wind. A massive limb was twisting — I could hear the tortured sound of it — and was about to fall.

"Marcus! You idiot! Get out of the way!" I screamed, more terrified now than angry; and I ran forward, scraping my knee on the edge of a toppled gravestone.

He heard my voice at last and turned his face toward me. Now I could see his desperate expression. He was sobbing.

"Louise! Help me!" he cried. I ran forward, dodging the debris that shot past me in the rushing water, which was now up to my knees. Above us, the tree limb groaned and shook.

"Run, Marcus! Come on!"

But he continued to stand there, immobile, sobbing. I was no more than three feet from him now, and it was difficult to stay upright in the rushing water.

"My foot is caught!" He grabbed my extended hand, but he couldn't move. I reached with my other hand through the cold swirling water and felt the rock; but it was a boulder, one of the huge stones from the wall. The river immediately beyond us was tossing them around as if they were weightless; but I couldn't move this one a single inch to free my brother.

We put our arms around each other, holding ourselves up together, and the water slapped now around my waist.

I heard the crack as the tree limb broke and began to fall. I closed my eyes and clutched Marcus. Then I felt myself lifted by water, turned and raked by branches, strangled by mud and twigs. The water churned over me until I thought I could hold my breath no longer; then my face scraped against rough rock, I was flung to the ground, the water receded, and I opened my eyes.

I was stunned, and dazed. But I was alive, and I was on the ground, lying in a few inches of water. I coughed, pushed myself painfully to a sitting position, and looked frantically for Marcus.

He was there, still, his slicker still a bright identifying mark, but we were far apart now. The falling tree had separated us and had freed him from the boulder, but the wave that had caused the tree to fall had also carried him out into the river. Now he was clinging to the tangle of branches that had once been the top of the ancient elm, and around him the river was at work, tearing off the leaves and bark.

The heavier end of the tree was still on the ground near me, partially submerged, but the force of the water was lifting it rhythmically and sucking away the earth beneath. I threw myself on it to hold it still, but the weight of my body was no match for the surge of water, and it continued to lift and pound as if I weren't there.

"Climb in on the tree, Marcus!" I shouted, but the words were barely said when I felt the entire heavy trunk lift under me, flinging me aside. Dislodged from the ground, it moved on the water. Some of its branches now ripped loose and shot away, disappearing almost instantly in the river.

I watched Marcus shift and move in the end of the broken tree. He inched closer toward the land, but he was still far away, and the massive trunk was floating now, beginning to move outward. I grabbed it, uselessly trying to hold it there with all my strength; but my strength was human, and the force of the flooding river was beyond anything human. The tree moved away from me as I watched helplessly, and my brother scrambled precariously in its tearing branches.

"Move back where it's safe, Louise!" I heard suddenly from behind me. "I'll get him!"

It was Tom. In a daze I turned and saw him throwing off his coat; his bike was on its side in the water where the cemetery path had been. He pushed past me roughly, waded between the boulders, and entered the river, guiding himself by holding the tree. He was moving in the same direction as the raging current, and it swept him quickly out toward Marcus. I watched as he grasped Marcus by the neck of his yellow slicker, pulled him into the water, and then, still holding the tree, started back, pulling Marcus behind him.

But the tree had been moving slowly all the time. Now there was an expanse of surging water between the land and the ugly, ripped trunk. And the current was against Tom now. I could see him fighting it, moving inch by inch, holding Marcus tightly. The tree bobbed, and moved out another foot. My brothers were moving in — but not fast enough. They advanced a few inches; the tree shifted and moved out farther.

Behind them, suddenly, I saw another huge, swirling wave approaching. I screamed, pointing, and Tom turned, saw the wall of brown water, and hugged Marcus to him. It was moving toward the land, the way the last one, the one that had caught Marcus and me, had; I watched as it captured my brothers, wrenched them loose from the drifting tree, and propelled them forward. It broke in front of me, bubbled around my feet, and deposited Marcus nearby. He raised himself to his hands and knees and vomited. I sobbed in relief.

But when I looked around through my tears and the rain that still was coming down, I saw that Tom was not there. Only Marcus had been swept ashore. I searched the landscape for my older brother, and finally I found him. He had been sucked back by the reversal of the wave, and now he was out there, clinging to what remained of the tree. As Marcus and I watched in horror, the explosive current in the river caught the tree and Tom, turned them in a sweeping circle, and sent them swiftly out to the center of the widening, treacherous river; then, bobbing wildly, they disappeared around the bend to the south.

13

I turned and looked once more at Marcus, who was still on his knees in the shallow water, choking and retching. He was battered, bruised, and scared; but he was alive. And I was sure that Tom was not.

I turned and ran, leaving Marcus there. It seemed as if I had been running through this rain all day. This time, as I ran splashing and sobbing through the cemetery, my feet were bare; somehow my boots and shoes had been wrested from my feet by the river. And my slicker was in shreds, the hat gone. I pushed my wet hair out of my eyes, wincing when I touched my face. I pulled my hand away; it was covered with blood.

I tried, as I ran, to remember which way to turn as I left the cemetery gate: Which way would be closest to a house where I could use the telephone and call for help?

But close to the cemetery entrance, I saw a man kneeling on one of the small rises that was still free of the flood. I didn't care who he was, or that he seemed to be praying for a lost relative or friend. He was a man — an adult — and I was a child with one brother still in a battered heap by the devastated wall and the other lost in that ghastly, grabbing water. I ran, gasping, up the small hill to beg him to help me.

He stood and backed off when he saw me. "Go away!" he said harshly.

I realized how frightening I must seem, covered with mud and bleeding from the gash in my forehead, appearing out of nowhere in that godforsaken place inundated now with turbulent water and broken tombstones. But I recognized the man. It was Kenny Stratton's father.

"It's me, Mr. Stratton," I cried, desperate. "It's Louise Cunningham — I'm Kenny's friend. Help me! My brother got sucked into the river!"

He stared at me with panic in his eyes. "Where?" he asked.

"Down there!" I pointed. "He's caught on a tree, and it headed down that way, toward the bridge!"

"I'll call the police," he said. "Come with me!"

He dropped a small object he was holding, and turned and ran toward the cemetery gate. Without thinking, I picked up the small, mud-coated thing and thrust it into the pocket of my slicker. His legs were much longer than mine; I followed him at a distance, then saw him bang on the door of a house and go inside.

Panting, I reached the house and climbed the front steps just as he came back out. "The police already know," he said. "Someone spotted him from the bridge when he got caught on one of the supports. They're trying to get him out now."

People came from inside the house and clustered around me. Someone wiped at my bloody face with a towel, but I pushed her away.

"I have my car right here," Mr. Stratton told me. "I'll take you down to the bridge where he is."

"Is Tom dead?" I asked.

No one answered for a moment. "They don't know," Mr. Stratton said, finally, and put his arm around me.

"You go on," I said. "I have to go back. My other brother's still down there."

"Another brother?" asked the woman who had been trying to wipe my face. "Is he all right?"

"He's puking," I said flatly, "and I want to take him home."

They let me go. I looked back, as I reentered the cemetery, and saw that they had all gone with Mr. Stratton to the old car that was parked in the rain-filled street.

This time I half-walked, half-ran, into the cemetery, following the same flooded path through the same eerie, desolate landscape. When I was partway to the river, I saw Marcus in his bright yellow slicker, or what remained of it, coming slowly toward me. He was limping. Like me, he was barefoot and bleeding and coated with mud; like me, he was crying.

"Tom's caught in the bridge supports and they're trying to get him out," I said when I reached him.

Marcus didn't answer. He stared at me with stunned eyes. His nose was bleeding, and the blood turned pink as it was diluted on his face by rain and tears. The pale pink drops fell from his chin.

"Come on, Marcus. We have to go home and tell Mother."

He still said nothing. He stared at me and wept silently. I was frightened by his silence; I wished he would scream or hit me. Instead, he simply stood there, dazed.

Finally he looked down at his own hand, clenched to a fist around a piece of bent and twisted metal. He raised his hand, opened his fist, and handed the odd-shaped thing to me. It was what was left of Tom's glasses.

Then he spoke. "His bike is there," he said.

"I know. Father will get it. Come."

But still he didn't move.

Finally I shook him. "Marcus!" I said. "Marcus the Newbold! Let's go *home*."

He followed me then. We stumbled toward home, and the rain continued to fall.

The doctor came to the house and examined Marcus and me as we sat shuddering, silent and stunned. He cleaned our cuts, bandaged Marcus's ankle, and gave us both pills that made us sleep most of the day and night. In the morning I felt groggy and confused. Mother told me what had happened, but I shrank inside myself and wouldn't listen. I refused to look at the newspaper. On the front page there was a picture of men lifting my brother carefully to the bridge with ropes. I turned away from it, feeling sick, and stared dumbly at the wall.

"Louise," Mother said in a firm voice, holding my shoulders, "read what it says. BOY SURVIVES FLOOD MISHAP. Tom isn't dead, Louise."

I believed her, but it didn't seem to matter. Mother and Father had been at the hospital all night long. Tom was in a coma.

The tree, with Tom clinging to it, had been swept down to the bridge in just seconds and had caught there. He had screamed for help and been heard. But the water washed over him in surges, slamming him again and again into the concrete and steel supports. By the time help reached him, he was battered and unconscious, half-drowned, with both arms and his skull fractured. Even the doctors were not sure if he would live.

But Mother was sure. She said so with brisk authority: Tom would live. She made us all believe it.

Father's sisters, Florence and Jeanette, arrived by train and took up residence in our house, caring for Stephanie while Mother and Father spent days at the hospital beside Tom's bed. My aunts saw to it that Marcus and I got dressed and off to school in the mornings after we were ready to go back. Marcus's badly sprained ankle healed; our cuts and bruises healed; we were the center of attention for a while at school. And, after a few days, the rain even stopped.

But Tom didn't heal. His broken bones, the X rays showed, were beginning to knit together inside the heavy plaster casts. But he didn't wake up. After a week, even Mother's vibrant optimism became shaky, and sometimes I saw her stop whatever she was doing and stand silently, a look of infinite sadness on her face.

Father, too, was changed. His usual attitude of gruff playfulness and good-natured rudeness evaporated. He was gentle toward Mother and tolerant of the intrusion of the two aunts, who were always in the way and creating complicated productions of the most simple household tasks.

"Relax," he said to Aunt Florence, who came to him, worried and flustered, one evening when Mother was at the hospital. Stephanie's only clean pajamas had a broken elastic in the waist. "Use a safety pin," Father told her calmly. Marcus and I overheard and looked at each other in astonishment. In the old days — before the flood, as we referred to that time to each other — he would have exploded; he would have bellowed, "For the Lord's sake, Florence, put the child to bed naked! Do you think the world requires a piece of elastic to revolve? And stop that incessant hand-wringing or you'll drive me completely around the bend!"

Another evening I went to the basement to borrow the ball of twine that I knew was on Father's workbench, and I found him there, all alone. Around him, strewn across the workbench and on the floor, were all the parts of Tom's bike. He was meticulously examining each piece, one by one; he was sanding and scraping bits of rust away and rubbing the pieces with oil. It was the kind of thing that Thomas himself would have done, but Father had always been too impatient for such intricate, time-consuming tasks. He hadn't heard me come down, and he didn't see me watching. For a long time I stood there in the shadow of the huge furnace, and watched as he held the smallest bolts almost lovingly in his large hands, smoothing and oiling them, fitting the pieces together so that the bicycle would be whole again.

Some nights after supper he sat quietly in his big chair, ignoring the evening paper; and if we went to him, Marcus or Stephie or I, he would take us into his lap and stroke our hair in silence.

After three weeks, Mother told Marcus and me that we could go to the hospital to see Tom. We were too young, and it was against the rules; but they would make an exception for us. We went with her in the afternoon, after school, and we were frightened. In the hospital room, Marcus and I stood beside each other and looked apprehensively at the bandaged stranger in the bed.

"Thomas," Mother said, leaning over him and

speaking in her normal, everyday voice, "it's a beautiful day, and I saw a bright red cardinal in the yard this morning.

"And today I've brought Marcus and Louise to see you," she added cheerfully.

She nudged us forward. "Say hello to him," she said.

"Hello, Tom," I whispered.

"Hi," Marcus said.

"Tell him what's going on in school," Mother suggested.

Talking to someone whose eyes were closed and who didn't respond made me uncomfortable and scared. But I took a deep breath and said, "Today we played softball at recess and Charlie Clancy got picked off second base when he tried to steal third. And, let's see, ah, Nancy Brinkerhoff has chicken pox, but Mother says we all had it when we were little, so we can go down to her house after school and play with her." I poked Marcus, so that he would take over.

"We had a spelling bee," Marcus said, "and I missed 'receive,' like I always do. What else? Oh yes, Kenny Stratton had to stay after school because he wrote a swear word inside his arithmetic book and the teacher saw it, and —"

He looked at Mother. "I can't think of anything else," he said apologetically.

At the end of our brief and miserable visit, Mother walked us to the elevator. She would stay until suppertime, and Marcus and I could go on home. We both tried to think of something cheerful to say.

"I think his bandages are neat," Marcus said. "I always wished I could have a broken arm so that I could have a cast and people could sign their names on it."

"Yeah. Me, too," I said.

Suddenly Marcus's eyes filled with tears. "He looks *dead*!" he wailed.

Mother put her arm around him. She led both of us into a small waiting room nearby. "He's just asleep," she said. "That's what a coma is, you know. I explained that to you — it's a very, very deep sleep."

Marcus's outburst had freed my own tears, and now I cried, too. "Why do you keep talking to him? Why did you make us *talk* to him? That felt terrible!"

She sat us both down, and she sat beside us on the stiff, uncomfortable couch. "The doctors told Father and me," she explained, "that although they can't be sure, they think that sometimes a person in a coma can hear. Tom can't open his eyes yet, and he can't speak, of course, but maybe he can hear us. So I talk to him all day, and Father does, too, when he's here."

I thought about what an agonizing effort it had been for me to say a few sentences to Tom. "Don't you get tired?"

It was a foolish question because I could see how tired she was. It showed in her eyes.

"Yes," she said. "Of course I do. It's hard to think of things to say, all day long. But I keep talking because it may be the thing that wakes him up."

I wiped my eyes with the back of my hand. "I could try harder," I said. "I promise I will. Can I come back, if I promise to try harder?"

Marcus nodded in agreement. "I will, too," he said.

And so the schedule changed. Every day, after school, Marcus and I trudged to the hospital, so that Mother could go home and rest. Every day until suppertime, Marcus and I stood beside that bed and talked endlessly. We became accustomed to it, the bizarre act of talking to a motionless, sleeping figure in a bed. We told jokes, sang songs, made up stories, and recalled the plots of movies. Nurses came and went, adjusting Tom's covers, taking his pulse and his blood pressure; they smiled at us, and nodded their approval. And we talked on.

Days passed, and spring turned into summer. Still Tom didn't wake.

14

One day another postcard came from Claude, who in his rootless travels had not heard about Tom's tragedy. It was addressed to Marcus and me, and postmarked Cheyenne, Wyoming.

I hadn't thought about Claude in a long time, and now the postcard made me angry. "This is the land where fortunes are to be maid," it read, "and I am in on the ground floor of something. One of these days I will ride up in a Rolls Roice and take you two for SOME RIDE!!!"

I showed it to Marcus, who shrugged, and then I showed it to Mother. She laughed.

"There he goes again," she said. "Claude will still be chasing his dreams when he's ninety years old."

I crumpled the stiff postcard in my hands and threw it into the wastebasket disdainfully. "I hate him," I said. "He lied to Marcus and me."

She was still laughing. "Don't say that, Louise. He told you fairy tales, perhaps. But he never meant to lie. When people tell wild stories, they don't expect anyone to believe them."

"Oh no? How about what he told Marcus and me, that he'd hidden something for us — a gift just for us two?"

"He probably did. Probably somewhere in the house, eventually, you'll find some silly gift and realize that it came from Claude."

"I'm not talking about some silly gift. He told us what it *was*. And he said it came from Russia, that he'd smuggled it out. It was fancy Easter eggs, all decorated with real jewels, even diamonds. And we believed him. Remember that crazy clue he left, those words that don't mean anything? He made it all up!"

"My goodness, Louise, I forgot to tell you something. I remembered the instant you said Easter eggs. It's been here for *days*, and I completely forgot — I'm sorry." She went to the hall closet and reached up to the shelf.

"Here," she said, handing it to me. "I was in the library, and Mr. Mueller asked me to bring this home for you. He said he was sorry it took so long, but he had to order it from the state library."

I took the small book and looked at the picture on the cover. Then I leafed through and looked briefly at the other pictures. There they were: those fabulous, priceless eggs that Claude had described.

Some of the photographs were in color, and the brilliance of the jewels gleamed on the pages.

I tossed the book scornfully on the kitchen table. "Those are the eggs that he said he had hidden for us, the liar," I said.

Mother picked it up and turned the pages. "They're very beautiful," she said.

"And he lied, right?" I looked belligerently at her. "He couldn't have gotten two of those for Marcus and me, could he?"

She was reading some of the captions. After a moment she put the book back down. "No," she told me, "I'm sure he couldn't have. But, Louise —"

"What?" I asked sullenly.

"He *wanted* to. Can't you be grateful for that, that Uncle Claude wanted to give you something exquisite and valuable?"

"No. And I hate him, for making me believe it."

"He has flaws, Louise, like all the rest of us."

"Claude the Flawed," I said bitterly.

"Louise, listen to me," Mother said firmly. "You know Claude is different. You know he has flaws. He can't seem to hold a job, he has no money, and sometimes he drinks too much. But he never hurts anyone. He tries so hard, still, to create worlds for himself, worlds where he is rich and where he can give wonderful gifts. It's all in his imagination — but imagination itself is a gift, Louise. Can't you appreciate that, at least?"

I shook my head stubbornly. "Why don't you

hate him?" I asked. "You've known him his whole life, and he probably lied to you all the time. He probably made up all sorts of stuff, and you probably believed him lots of times when you were young."

She smiled. "Sometimes I did."

"So there. You ought to hate him."

"Louise, Louise," Mother said, "he's my *brother*. I've always loved him."

Marcus and I stood by Tom's bed late in the afternoon. We were exhausted with the effort of talking continuously, as we always were at the end of the day. There was a moment's pause as we both searched our minds for something new to say.

I remembered the newspaper, Tom's greatest love, his ambition for the future.

"Father says they miss you at the paper," I said, taking a deep breath to embark on another lengthy one-way speech. "They got so used to you always hanging around and helping out, that now they really miss you.

"On the morning after the flood, your picture was on the first page; did Mother or Father tell you that? We saved it so you can see it when you wake up.

"And stupid Alexandra Marek's picture was on the front page of the paper the day before, remember? And all her dumb cows? So she was all prepared to be really stuck-up about it, but nobody even noticed it by the time she was back in school, because by then *your* picture had been there, and yours was much bigger and more interesting."

I paused, and Marcus took over, telling Tom of something I had forgotten. "And right in the middle of all of that about the flood," Marcus said, "the police found some of the Leboffs' silverware — a dozen forks, with a special *L* on them for Leboff — at a pawn shop in Westover. So they think the thief was heading west and just stopped to sell them there before he went on. The guy who gave him money for them notified the police later, but he couldn't really describe the thief; he just said it was an ordinary-looking man.

"But here's the funny thing, Tom," Marcus went on. "Everybody had forgotten the robbery by then, because of the flood, so the story about the forks was just a little thing on one of the back pages. Father said if it hadn't been for the flood, it would have made page one."

Marcus stopped talking for a minute, and we both watched Tom. But he didn't change. He was thinner, now, and looked more like a little boy than the young man he had been. His face was very pale. The sheet over his chest moved slowly as he breathed. His breaths were the long, silent breaths of someone barely alive.

"Tom," I said suddenly, "Marcus and I think Uncle Claude stole the Leboffs' silver. Marcus and I knew where the key was, remember? And nobody knows this, but we showed Claude. And Claude is a rat and a rotten liar. He's a fraud, just like you said. You were right about Uncle Claude, Tom, and we haven't decided for sure yet, but maybe Marcus and I are going to tell on him someday.

"I hate him," I added, "and Marcus hates him, too."

But there was no response from Tom — we had learned by now not to expect one — and it was time to go home.

Marcus leaned over and began talking into Tom's silent, expressionless face again. "Claude left this message for Louise and me, in code, and we thought it really meant something. We used to say it to each other, just in private, all the time, and sometimes we wrote it to each other and poked it through this hole we have in the wall between our rooms."

We were telling Tom all of our secrets. It had been so important to Marcus and me, to have secrets together, and now it seemed important to tell them all to Tom.

"*Ya tebya lyublyu*," I said.

"*Ya tebya lyublyu*," Marcus repeated.

We said it in unison, and I think we had both meant to laugh at it and at ourselves, so that somewhere down there in his sleep, where maybe he could hear and understand, Tom could laugh at it and at us, too.

But we kept saying it and didn't laugh. It had meant so much to us, those meaningless and mysterious words; for a while it had been such a strong and secret bond. Now we were sharing it with our brother who seemed lost, drowned for a second time in the deepness of this horrible sleep.

"*Ya tebya lyublyu, ya tebya lyublyu*," we chanted together, leaning over his bed. The evening nurse appeared, coming to take over from the afternoon shift, and she looked at us curiously. We didn't care. We ignored her, said the magic words one more time, and then went home for dinner.

That night, after I was in bed, I heard the knock on the wall that Marcus and I had devised as a signal. Marcus was about to send a note through our message hole. I turned on my light and reached for the paper that appeared.

DO YOU THINK HE STILL HAS DREAMS? Marcus had written to me.

I grabbed my pencil and wrote a lengthy answer while Marcus waited on the other side of the wall.

YES, I wrote, MOTHER SAID HE'LL STILL BE CHASING HIS DREAMS AROUND WHEN HE'S NINETY YEARS OLD, AND YOU KNOW WHAT I THINK? I THINK THAT'S STUPID. HE'S A LIAR AND A FRAUD AND A SILVERWARE THIEF AND I HOPE HE NEVER COMES BACK. AND ALSO HE CAN'T SPELL. ROLLS ROICE, HA HA.

I shoved my response through the hole and waited, but Marcus sent no note back. I turned off my light again. But I heard a noise in Marcus's room. I listened. Marcus was crying.

I climbed out of bed, went to the hall, and opened Marcus's door. He was in bed, his arms around his pillow, his shoulders shaking.

"Marcus, what's wrong?" I asked him.

"I meant Tom," he wept.

15

Stephie chattered endlessly at breakfast, about everything, and my two aunts bustled here and there, worrying about this and that: "Do you think this toaster needs repairs? I don't like the looks of that last piece of toast — it's much darker than it should be. And I believe I smell something odd from the toaster. Do you think it needs repairs, Florence?" "Well now, Jeanette, I just don't know. Shall we ask Hallie or Matt? I hate to disturb them with these household things, after all they're going through, but you know a defect in an electrical appliance can be dangerous. Goodness, what if Stephanie touched it and there were some defect that might cause her harm — Stephanie, dear, promise me that you will never touch this toaster; I think it may be defective."

Even Stephie had learned to tune them out and ignore their endless laments and warnings and complaints. She continued to talk to her doll.

Father came into the kitchen, poured himself some coffee, and drank it standing up. He couldn't bear to eat breakfast at home anymore; he said that if he had to listen to Florence and Jeanette first thing in the morning, he would go stark, raving mad.

"Let your mother sleep late, pip-squeaks," he said. "She had trouble sleeping last night. She's upset about something."

"About Tom?" I asked, suddenly frightened. "He was just the same when we saw him yesterday."

"No. I was with him last night, and there's no change. I don't know what's bothering her. She'll probably be all over it when she gets up." He set his cup down and turned to leave for the office.

"Oh, say," he said as he picked up his briefcase in the hall, "Marcus and Louise. Here's a mystery that you can clear up for me. I hate to start a day with an unsolved mystery."

"What's that?" We went into the hall to kiss him good-by and to solve his mystery.

"Last night, when I was at the hospital, the night nurse was there — you know, that heavyset woman with gray hair? I forget her name."

"Yeah," I said. "She came on duty just before we left."

"Well, she said that she was very surprised to hear you two speaking in Russian to your brother. I had to admit I was surprised, too. Where on earth did you pick up any Russian?"

Marcus and I looked at each other in amazement.

"It's *Russian*?" Marcus asked.

"Apparently whatever you were saying to Tom was Russian," Father said, grinning. "Didn't you know?"

We shook our heads. "What does it mean? We thought it was just words that didn't mean anything! Did she tell you what it means?" We were both talking at once.

But he shook his head. "I didn't think to ask her that."

"Call her! Ask her!" We tugged at him, pleading.

He looked at his watch. "She's gone off duty by now."

"Call her at home!" I begged.

"I don't know her name. Do you remember her name?"

But Marcus and I were at a loss. We paid no attention to the names of the nurses.

"Well," he said, turning to leave, "your mother will know. You can ask her when she gets up. But let her sleep for a while. She really had a rough night."

Marcus and I waited impatiently, prowling the house aimlessly, until Mother woke. School had ended for the year; outside, we could hear the neighborhood kids playing in the street. Nancy Brinkerhoff and Ben Staley came to the door to ask us to join a game of hide-and-seek, but we said no. We waited. Finally, at ten, we heard Mother go to the kitchen and pour herself some coffee.

Marcus and I ran to the kitchen. "Mother!" I said eagerly. "Guess what!"

But her face was grim. "Louise," she said in a cold voice, "come upstairs with me. I have to talk to you."

"But, Mother! Marcus and I —"

"Louise. Come *now*."

I followed her upstairs, motioning to Marcus to wait.

She took me into her room. The bed was still unmade; she sat down on it with her shoulders slumped as if she were very sad or in pain. I stood dutifully in front of her, waiting to be scolded or punished for some unknown offense, and she put her arms around me and held me very tight. Then she released me, and said, "Louise, you're my oldest daughter, and I love you more than I can ever tell you. Whatever happens, I want you to know that."

"I do," I said, puzzled. "I've always known that."

"And we must try our best to be honest with each other, always," she said.

I thought of Claude and wondered if he had tried his best. But I nodded. "Okay," I said.

She reached into the pocket of her bathrobe, took something out, and handed it to me. "I want you to tell me exactly where and how you got this," she said.

I held it, looked at it, and turned it over and over in my hands. It was a small silver pitcher, with an elegant, scrolled *L* engraved on its side. I knew intuitively that it was a piece of the Leboffs' stolen silver. But I had never seen it before in my life.

"It's not mine," I said in confusion. "This is the first time I've ever seen it."

Mother sighed. "Louise," she said firmly, "last night I went out to the shed to bring in some gardening tools because I was going to try to find time to weed the tulip beds this morning. And there, lying in the corner, were your slickers — yours and Marcus's. They'd been there ever since that terrible day when Tom was hurt. And I thought that finally, after all this time, I could bring myself at least to pick them up and throw them away in the trash can."

She looked for a long time at the little pitcher before she went on. "This was in the pocket of your slicker," she said.

"Mother," I told her, "I'm telling you the truth. I've never seen it before. I didn't put it there."

Solemnly I crossed my heart. I looked at her face, sad and frustrated, and I thought of how hard it must have been for her to pick up those two torn, bloodstained slickers and to be reminded of what had happened to us and, especially, to Tom. The terror of that day surfaced in my memory, and I thought of how I had run through the rain, how I had seen Marcus's yellow slicker so bright against the terrible brown river; I thought of how I had screamed and sobbed, running there among the toppled tombstones, and — then I remembered.

"Mother," I said urgently, "it was Mr. Stratton! He dropped it on the ground, when I screamed for him to help me, and I picked it up and ran after him. I wasn't even thinking about anything but Tom. It was all covered with mud, and I didn't know what it was. Mr. Stratton had it there with him — he was up on this little hill, sort of hunched down, and I thought he was praying. He was *digging*, Mother! He dug this up from the ground in the cemetery!"

We hugged each other in relief. "I'll tell your father," she said. "He'll call the police."

I followed her down the stairs as she went to the phone. "Mother, what's the name of Tom's night nurse? The one with the gray hair?"

"Mira," she said distractedly. "Mira Leonov."

I didn't even listen to her conversation with Father. I took the telephone book, and Marcus and I found Leonov listed there. The house was on Woodmont Street, only a few blocks away from ours. We ran outside and headed for the night nurse's house.

The man who answered the door of the small frame house smiled pleasantly at us, but couldn't understand what we were saying. He spoke practically no English. He stood there patiently, listening, watching our lips as if it might help, but finally he simply began to laugh heartily.

"Quit trying to explain everything, Marcus," I suggested. "Let me try saying something real simple."

"Mira Leonov," I said to the man, and he nodded. "Is she here?"

He seemed to understand, but his face wrinkled up with the effort as he tried to think of an answer for us. Finally he resorted to pantomime; he put his hands together in a praying position, arranged them beside his face, against his cheek, closed his eyes, and snored loudly. Then he opened his eyes and beamed.

"She's asleep," Marcus said in disgust.

"Well, she works all night," I said, defending poor Mira Leonov.

"Let's tell him to wake her up."

"How?"

Neither of us could figure out how to say "Wake her up, please, it's important" in sign language. The man stood there smiling at us, waiting. He seemed to be just as frustrated as we were.

"Well, look, Louise," Marcus suggested, "he's probably her husband, don't you think?"

I nodded. "You — Mr. Leonov?" I asked.

He smiled and nodded eagerly.

"So he speaks Russian," Marcus said to me. "He'll know what it means."

"Great; how's he going to tell *us*?"

"Let's try, anyway."

I shrugged; it couldn't hurt. Marcus and I stood up straight as if we were reciting in school, side by side. He said it first, pronouncing it carefully; and then I repeated it.

"*Ya tebya lyublyu.*"
"*Ya tebya lyublyu.*"

The man's smile broadened in delight, and he clapped his hands together. He knelt, there in the open doorway, so that his face was level with ours.

"*Ya tebya lyublyu,*" he said in a booming voice, and he opened his arms wide and drew us both into them. We were squished against his chest, but it wasn't a bad or a frightening feeling; the man seemed so happy.

He let us go and pinched our cheeks gently. Then, still kneeling at our level, he took a deep breath, and it was obvious that he was about to attempt a translation.

"*Ya tebya lyublyu,*" he said. "Russian."

We nodded.

He grinned. "English," he announced proudly.

We waited, while he thought it over.

"I love you!" he said.

We backed away, startled.

"Thank you," I said, nervously. "Good-by now." Marcus and I headed down the steps of the small porch, and he watched us, beaming.

"I love you!" he called, and we both nodded, embarrassed, and waved to him.

We walked home together sheepishly, hoping no one had seen or overheard our encounter.

"Jeez," Marcus muttered, kicking a stone down the sidewalk, "You don't say stuff like that to strangers."

"Well," I pointed out, "we said it to Tom. And Tom's like a stranger. I feel like I don't even know him anymore."

Marcus turned angrily and punched me on the arm. "You take that back," he said.

I didn't respond, except to rub the place where he had punched me, and he did it again, and repeated his words. "Take it back," he said. "Take it back."

But I wouldn't. I simply walked beside him silently, enduring his repeated jabs at my aching arm, not even bothering to punch him in return.

When we reached our house, the aunts were there on the porch, both talking at once, waving their arms and their aprons, giving us instructions and news and warnings and predictions. When we sorted out what they were saying, we shrieked with delight and headed full speed for the hospital, where Mother and Father were waiting for us. Tom was awake.

16

It was a long time before Tom was really well. He had to learn to walk and to talk and to read, as if his life had begun all over again. He didn't remember the day of the flood; when he came home from the hospital and we showed him his bike, newly painted after Father's hours of meticulous repairs, he seemed puzzled and confused. "Why did you do that?" he asked Father, forming the words very carefully. "It was okay before."

When we explained to him that the bike had been smashed by rocks and had lain in the filthy flood water for three days, he just shook his head.

"You take it, Marcus," he said, gesturing from his wheelchair to the bicycle. "You do my paper route until I'm better."

And Marcus, who once would willingly have undergone terrible tortures before getting up at dawn to ride a paper route, took over for Tom. He went to bed early each night so that he could wake up at five, and I missed the laughter late at night and the notes poked through our secret place.

Throughout the summer, our town was rebuilt and the damage from the flood repaired. It took many weeks to put the cemetery back together. Teams of burly workers, like ants inching bread-crumbs to their nest, moved the heavy gravestones from the places where they had been strewn by the flood and arranged them in rows to be returned to their proper locations. Downed trees were sawed into manageable lengths and hauled away; uprooted shrubbery was discarded and new grass was planted. Meticulously, the workers replaced the ruined wall. The entire cemetery was cordoned off with ropes and No Trespassing signs while the men labored there through the summer. But on a Wednesday afternoon, the ropes and barriers were opened and I went inside once again, this time with an escort of three policemen.

The landscape was changed, and I stood on the path — new gravel now — and looked around to get my bearings. Behind me was the gate. Ahead, where I could hear the thumping noises from the workers, was the wall. The path curved, and the land, bare now of gravestones, which were still waiting to be reset, looked unfamiliar.

My father was with us, and he could see my confusion. "Take your time, Louise," he said. "Let's start down by the river. I'll show you where I found Tom's bike."

And so he took me there, with the police following silently behind.

"Here," said Father, pointing to the spot. "Tom's bike was here."

I looked at the patch of bare earth. Behind me, I could hear the policemen shift their feet. One muttered to another, "That was his son, the boy who —"

"Marcus was over there," I said, and pointed. "He was throwing up. And that —" I pointed again, to the tree trunk scarred by a massive laceration in its side, "was the tree that fell."

Father nodded, and we both stared for a moment at the tree that had both nearly destroyed and possibly saved my brothers and me.

"I was here. And when I saw that Marcus was okay, I started to run to get help. I ran this way. I thought I was on the path, but it was all water, so I couldn't see."

I began to walk, and they followed me.

"I was heading for the gate, and I was trying to think which way to turn when I got to the street. I think — no, wait; I went *this* way. I remember going between these two trees."

I turned from the path and walked between the two huge trees, which still stood, firm and upright.

"There were some places that weren't under water," I said, "because they were higher. See over there? That little hill?"

Father nodded.

"That's not the one. I ran past that one, and over there, that second hill — that's the one where he was. I could barely see him because of the rain. At first I thought he was a statue. Then, when I realized it was a man, I thought he was praying."

We all headed for the second hill. "Did he see you, Louise?" one of the policemen asked.

"Yes, and he heard me, too, when I got close, because I was screaming. I scared him. He yelled at me to go away."

"Then what happened?"

"When I was close enough, I saw that it was Kenny Stratton's father. And I told him what had happened to Tom. He ran for help. He ran to that house over there, outside the gate."

"When did he drop the pitcher?"

"When he stood up and started to run. I didn't know what it was. I just picked it up and ran after him."

By now we were all standing on the side of the hill. The sun was hot, and the earth was solid, baked firm, but marked with the ravages of the rain. One of the policemen poked at the dry, hard dirt. He went to the top of the small rise and scraped with a stick until a flat stone marker was revealed.

"Mary Stratton," he said, reading the carved words. "He was digging in his own family's burial plot, for crissake."

The policeman who seemed to be the leader of the trio glanced down at the name. "He wasn't so dumb," he said. "Anybody seeing him digging here would think he was planting flowers or something. Maybe praying, like the girl thought.

"Let's rope this area off before we start digging." He was directing the other two men. "Mr. Cunningham," he said, turning to Father, "you can take your daughter home now. The county attorney will be in touch with you."

"Father," I said, as he and I walked toward the cemetery gate, "I can go home alone. You ought to stay, for the paper."

He stopped for a moment, looked back, and sighed. Then he put his arm around my shoulders. "I'll call them when I get back," he said. "I can send someone over to cover it. For once in my life, I think I'd just like to walk my daughter home."

On the day of Mr. Stratton's hearing, I was both terrified and proud because I was called to testify. My parents sat solemnly in the courtroom and watched as I perched on the witness stand in my best dress and answered the questions as carefully and honestly as I could.

When I had finished, and the judge smiled and said, "You may step down now, Louise," I hesitated. I had been looking at Mr. Stratton sitting there with his pinched face, so much like Kenny's, and he looked so ashamed and so scared.

I bit my lip. "Can I say something else?" I asked the judge in a whisper. He nodded.

"I know they found all the other stuff there, where it was buried," I said earnestly. "And my father told me that the man from the pawn shop identified Mr. Stratton, so I guess it's true that he stole all the silver. But I think it's important that when I screamed to him because my brother was drowning Mr. Stratton put the pitcher down and ran as fast as he could for help. He didn't even think twice. He helped me. And — well, that's all. I just think that's important."

"Thank you, Louise," the judge said. "We will certainly keep that in mind."

I told my father that I thought my picture should be on page one because I was a witness in the case; but he laughed and said he hoped there would never be a Cunningham on page one again.

One night, fooling around with Marcus in his room after supper, I said to him, "You know, Uncle Claude didn't steal the silver."

"I know that. If he had, old Kenny Stratton wouldn't have had to move to Cleveland to live with his grandparents. So what?"

"So I don't hate Uncle Claude anymore."

"I don't hate him either. I don't think I ever really did."

"And maybe he isn't a complete liar, like I thought."

"Maybe he'll drive up in a Rolls-Royce someday," Marcus suggested.

"And *maybe*, Marcus, he really did smuggle those eggs out of Russia —"

Marcus groaned. "Well, tough luck if he did. I'm sick of searching this house."

"Yeah, me, too, but I've decided it doesn't matter if we ever find them. It's like you said once, the whole house is special just because it might have a treasure in it."

"Also," Marcus pointed out, "he really does know Russian, Louisamanda."

"Yeah."

I could hear Tom across the hall in his room, walking heavily and slowly from his desk to his bed. One of his legs still dragged awkwardly, but he said he didn't mind; the doctors had promised that it would improve after a while. "Hey, Tom!" I called.

"What?"

"*Ya tebya lyublyu!*"

Tom's stern voice, so much like Father's, came back across the hall. "Marcus," he called, "and Louise. Can't you two obnoxious infants find something productive to do?"

Marcus and I dissolved in giggles.

Tom hadn't changed. Nothing had, really. But Marcus and I had changed in our knowledge of things. We loved Tom, and we had not truly known that before. And we knew now, really, that Claude had lied; but we accepted that, because Claude was different, because he was part of our family, and because he loved us.

Downstairs, we could hear Father muttering as he turned the pages of the paper, and Mother's low, expressive voice as she read a bedtime story to Stephanie. All around us, the house throbbed with the regular sounds of family life and of the love that bound us together, despite our flaws. The recognition of that was Claude's real gift — and, as Claude had said, it was a priceless one. But fragile? Claude was wrong about that. It was not fragile at all.